EULOGY

EULOGY

— *a novel* —

KEN MURRAY

TIGHTROPE BOOKS

2015

Tightrope Books
#207—2 College Street, Toronto, ON M5G 1K3
www.tightropebooks.com

Editor: Marnie Woodrow
Cover design: Deanna Janovski
Typography: Carleton Wilson

We thank the Canada Council for the Arts and the Ontario Arts
Council for their support of our publishing program.

Printed and bound in Canada

*This is a work of fiction. Any resemblance to actual persons living or dead
is purely coincidental.*

LIBRARY AND ARCHIVES CANADA CATALOGUING IN PUBLICATION

Murray, Ken, 1969-, author
    Eulogy / Ken Murray.

ISBN 978-1-926639-85-7 (pbk.)

    I. Title.

PS8626.U7755E94 2015   C813'.6   C2015-903350-0

For Emma
(and our mutual friend, Mr. Don Music)

PART ONE

ONE:

Toronto, December 2000—I visited my parents a few weeks before Christmas. Mom had left many messages, "William, where are you?" "William, are you okay?" "William, do you need any more Slender Nation?" I'd been ignoring her calls for months.

Terry had become a big part of my life, and I was happy. For the first time, I didn't want to be alone. I had my work at the Royal Ontario Museum, and she had hers in one of the bank towers downtown, and we had each other, and we had our music, and we fell into that inner space that people find when they love someone. Terry burned brightly in my world, and the rest of the world faded. Work was still good, but I fell out of touch with home, and for good reason; I didn't want to tell my parents about her because I didn't want to deal with their questions. I stopped calling, stopped visiting.

But dealing with it became inevitable: I had to tell my parents that I had a girlfriend, and even though I was a grown man with an established career, it was terrifying. I shouldn't have done it, but December has that magical power to make us that much more crazy. I drove home to

Otterton, the Southern Ontario industrial town where I grew up, for a Saturday lunch visit, blasting trance music along the way loud enough to make the steering wheel shudder.

Mom gave me a Slender Nation shake, as usual, and after I drank it she offered me a sandwich, while Dad sat grimly across from me. His short black hair, still neatly combed, was starting to grey, and I detected a hunch beginning to form in his shoulders.

"The government," he said, "is trying to destroy us."

"I know Dad, you've told me that before."

"You've got to be careful. Any day now, son, any day."

"Any day what?" I said, not sure if he was still talking of the government or had moved on to the Antichrist. The two were synonymous for him.

"They'll be coming for us. We don't have any good sense left in this country. We've got godless leaders. The States are doing much better—the new President Bush they've elected is a God-fearing man, he'll set things right. We need someone like him up here."

"Keith," barked Mom. "We must focus on the spirit." Mom adjusted her pink button, straightened her blouse, and instinctively touched her hair which, despite the years, remained as red as it was in my earliest memories of her.

"I am—this is all about the spirit. Everything is about the spirit," he said through clenched teeth. He pointed at her and said, "You have no idea."

"I have every idea," she said. "Or at least the good ones. Stop your negativity, now, I command it in the blood of Jesus." He wrung his hands at her and looked away. She turned to me, "Are you still drinking Slender Nation?" she said, her hands forming mirror C's in front of her.

"Yes," I said. "Actually, no. No I don't. I only drink it when I'm here, when you're in front of me, because that's what you want me to do."

"What are you saying?"

"I'm saying that I don't drink Slender Nation anymore."

"But you had some just now."

"I was being polite."

"So dishonesty is politeness? That's a lie, that's sin. You need to pray for forgiveness, right now."

"What would happen, William," said Dad, "if The Rapture came right now? You'd be left behind. We need to pray, together, as a family."

"No thanks," I said, feeling a surge of total honesty, the kind of honesty that has nothing to do with what's righteous or good. Righteousness may exist. And if it does, it moves quietly, anonymously, never calls itself by name.

"Please, let's pray. This is dangerous," said Mom, reaching for my hands.

"No." I got up, backed away from her.

"What's wrong with you?"

"Yes, what's wrong with you?"

"Nothing. Nothing at all. For the first time in my life

everything seems good, and you're jumping all over me."
I wanted—oh so much—to show them my life, perhaps
also to understand what had become of theirs, and desire
drowned the logic that said I should keep silent and let
them be.

"It's a woman, isn't it?" said Mom.

"The scarlet woman, God warns about her," said Dad.
Mom hit him. He sulked.

"It's not a woman," I said.

"So you don't have a girlfriend, still, at your age?"

"Which is it, Mom? Is it scary that I might have a girlfriend or is it weird that I don't?"

"Don't play games."

"I'm not. I'm just trying to know where you stand."

"So, there's a girl, then?"

"Actually, yes, there is a girl."

"So it's a woman, I knew it. Is she saved? Is she the one
who led you away from Slender Nation?"

"Who is she? Where's she from? Does she go to
church?" Dad was back in the conversation.

"When do we meet her?" said Mom, raising her voice.
I waited two full breaths before speaking.

"Her name is Terry." They were both leaning forward,
looking at me, and in their eyes I saw the fear and hunger, that maniac desire from which I'd been on the run
for most of my life. I told them more than they ever
wanted to hear: "She goes to church as much as I do,
that is to say, not at all." Mom turned pale. Dad looked

away. "I haven't eaten Slender Nation except in your presence since I was twelve, and I don't believe in your church."

Hoping to tell them about Terry, the best thing that had ever happened to me, I instead told them everything they'd refused to see, the facts I'd kept hidden in plain sight by living my quiet life and keeping them at a distance...

"It's important to meet your needs, but God says to do so in marriage, with one who is equal in belief," said Mom, in the voice of salesperson/counsellor.

"Yoke not yourself with an unbeliever!" When Dad paraphrased the Bible, he did so with English of the King James era.

"What do you think my needs are?" I said, but received only silence. Dad looked away, Mom crossed her arms. "I know how to meet my own needs," I said as I rolled up my sleeves and showed the fleshy carpets of scar that are my arms.

"Who did this to you?" said Dad.

"I did."

"Why?" said Mom.

"It's who I am."

"Blasphemy. You're sick!"

"So you do this instead of sex?" said Mom.

"For a long time, yes, this is what I did. But now we just have sex."

"How long has this been? When did you go astray?"

"It started right here," I said, "soon after Slender Nation and Jesus."

"In our house? You did this in our house?" She was rushing toward me, arm raised, but I didn't move, didn't duck. She stopped short. "You need to pray, pray right now!"

"You need to get out of that city," said Dad. "It's the gays getting married. I've seen it on the news. It's affecting you." He looked ill.

I left quickly, Mom following me down the driveway with a Bible and a can of Slender Nation. She wanted to instruct me on how to love, but she hadn't shared a bed or even a kind word with my father for nearly twenty years. I haven't one single memory of them kissing or even touching each other. All I ever saw between them was malice, barely contained. "It's not your fault," she said as I pulled away. "Your father never taught you to be a man."

Their sex made me, and maybe that was it.

I drove fast along the highway back to Toronto, the weight sinking in—I'd finally completed the split started all those years ago: paying lip service, since adolescence, to everything my parents expected while quietly, on the side, building my ordered yet desperate life.

When I first embraced pain, I would pinch myself, pull hairs, twist my skin, bruise myself slowly on my arms and legs, but always in a spot nobody could see. Over time, my habits evolved. It became a practice, my quiet way of getting by on my own. I kept to myself for so many years, never dated, never socialized beyond the decorum required of school and, later, work. When people insinuated about my sexual preference, I'd readily say, "I practice self-restraint."

Terry called as I drove. "How was your visit?" she said.

"Bad."

"Bad real bad, or just bad?"

"Bad real bad, I think."

She wanted me to come over but I said no. At home I drew a bath and turned the music loud. I was living in a converted garage in a back alley in the west end of town, where rents were cheaper. I kept my car and bicycle down below and lived in the loft above. Nobody was bothered by my noise. I turned it up until the shimmersound of electric beats dimpled the walls of my mind, and I sunk my head below the water, breathing deeply through my exposed mouth and nose, hearing the dampened shudderthrobs mix with heartbeats, and I slipped away.

When I pulled myself free of the water, it had grown cold. I saw the blood. In my calming, I had scratched open the scars on one of my arms. My fingers were bleeding. Next to the tub was an X-Acto blade. I don't remember doing it, but I'd given myself knifepoint cuts on my fingertips.

I jumped from the tub and cleaned up, carrying the blade between outstretched fingers to the kitchen garbage. I work with knives all the time.

I hate knives.

The phone rang. It was Terry. "You okay?" she said.

"No."

"I'll come over."

"No. Don't."

"What's wrong?" she said. I pulled the phone away for a moment, looked at the bloodstains on the counter, and remembered the hungry terror at the centre of my soul hearing those sermons when I was a kid.

"We have to stop," I said. "You and I. We have to stop. Things are going wrong, and we have to stop. It's been really good, but now it stops."

"You serious?"

"Yes."

"I suppose you expect me to cry and say you're wrong?"

"I've no expectations."

"Good. Did your parents put you up to this?"

"That's mean. My parents are done. Through. I'll never speak to them again."

"I don't understand."

"There's nothing to understand, Terry. This is what is."

"This sucks."

"We always said we were free to go, whenever. You said it would end with me cheating, that every relationship ends with the guy cheating. I didn't do that."

"Thanks. Thanks so much. You didn't cheat because you didn't know how. This is a brutal way to break up."

"I don't know how to do these things."

"My fault for getting together with an adult school-boy." She hung up.

It was over. I had never felt so alone, if that was possible. It seemed right, painful and right. I bandaged my arms, watched the news.

A few weeks later was the first time in my life I didn't go home for Christmas.

I didn't patch things up with Terry either. All I did was work, every day, in the conservation lab at the museum. I would have worked Christmas Day if I could have. Work was the best way to avoid the craving for pain.

It was also the best way to avoid the calls from my parents.

It was the best way to forget, but that's always been my problem. I have a hard time forgetting.

TWO:

Toronto, January 2001—A renewed barrage of calls and pleas from my parents in the new year led me to block their number. I came home one day to find them in my alley, in a prayer vigil with four others from their church. They were huddled, arms around each other, moaning in prayer at my door as I approached quietly on my bicycle. When I asked them to leave they started to lay hands on me. I pushed past, fumbled open the door as they grabbed at me and prayed in tongues. I shut the door on them. They pounded on it.

"Is *she* in there?" Mom yelled. "Let us in so we can pray."

"This would never have happened," Dad said to her, "if you hadn't been so miserable to him."

I called the police.

My name was promptly attached to a church-wide (and then world-wide-web-wide) prayer group:

> *Please pray for our son William, in Toronto, who has become a sexual deviant, mired in the clutch of Satan. We pray that he will not hurt anyone.*

Janet Oaks, Otterton, Ontario.

So good of her to spare my identity by not posting my full name, but still including her own. In a follow-up post, she gave out my work email address. I got my first clue of what she'd done when my inbox at work received the following:

> Hot man Bill,
> I am your sexual Jesus. Mother's anxiety WILL be relieved. Come onto me and you SHALL be set free.
> Yours,
> Lovelyone.

Lovelyone was the first of many. Here's a sampling:

> William, repent!
> Judgment will fall upon you, sinner. Give up your awfull [sic] labidinouness [sic] or face the fires of Hell!
> Righteous in Rochester

> Die. Fucking Queer.
> Jonathan

I can save you honey, you'll know only pleasure, no pain.

    Carly

Dear Mr. Oaks,

    It has come to my attention that your soul is in need of salvation. If I may be of service in leading you back to the Lord, my number is XXX-XXX-XXXX.

    Wilf Allman

    PS Please do not call after 8 pm.

The messages of love and hate kept coming, along with earnest pleadings, gleefully predicting my looming eternity in Hell. Sometimes, after deleting thirty or forty messages en masse, I'd get a mild kick from the thought of a lonely church outpost—in Kazakhstan, northern Manitoba, Vancouver, Guadalupe, or Korea—where people gathered in circles, bent kneed, eyes scrunched, all energy focused on fixing faraway people like me.

Search engines today still turn up my name for prayer, on websites from Argentina to Iceland, Alabama to Albania.

My lawyer's letter to Hillsview Independent Pentecostal Church, and to my parents, asking each to cease and desist, was a last resort (something I did only after phoning them and having Mom repeatedly ask me to repent. How could I humiliate her like this? Why didn't I come back to Slender Nation? Surely all the people at the museum could use it. Aren't there chubby curators?). Mom didn't see any irony when I pointed out she caused the humiliation herself by spreading the word.

"But what, you want me to keep it a secret when there are so many people who want to help you?"

THREE:

Toronto, April 2001—"Are you serious?" I said again, the phone suddenly hot against my ear.

"Yes."

"Really?" I steadied myself with a hand on my lab table.

From the other end of the line Adam, the long-suffering security guard, sighed and said, for the third time, "There are two people here to see you. They're waiting at the back entrance. And, yes, it's serious."

My parents had come to my work. It had to be them, I never received unannounced visitors. As always, they were trying to save me, but coming here was too much. They'd gone too far.

I carefully set my work aside, a book printed in 1753—pigskin bound and yellowing—for which I was testing the chemical composition of the binding.

My official title at the Royal Ontario Museum is Paper Conservator, Books (not to be confused with Paper Conservator, Art). I also dabble in wood when called upon, but there are others who are more expert in this area. My day to day is to keep old books healthy: prevent paper decay, repair papers, parchments, and scrolls that are damaged, and to do all this in a way that doesn't compromise the integrity or historic value of the pieces. I work meticulously and by my work these objects are preserved and sometimes displayed. The work allows me to keep to myself, except for the occasional visit from a curator.

Quickly, I made my way down five flights of stairs. I avoided elevators, less chance of having to make conversation with people.

My parents had left the crappy little town where I grew up, drove all the way to the city they hate, and had shown up at my workplace to harass me. I needed to find a way to be rid of them, but also to avoid a scene. The intrusion was intolerable. For all I knew, they were already trying to sell Adam the security guy on the life-giving value of Slender Nation or having another one of their blowout arguments with each other.

I burst from the stairwell and rounded the corner toward the security desk to face them.

There I was met by two police officers, one a younger man, the other an older woman. "William Oaks?" she said.

"Yes."

They introduced themselves, and then she said, "May we speak with you in private?"

"What's this about?" My mind raced through possibilities, but my worst vice, on the legal side, was Napster. I couldn't think of a possible accusation they might have.

"This is best discussed in private," said the man.

Something tweaked inside me. "No thanks. Whatever you want to say or ask, do it here."

They looked at each other uncomfortably. She nodded. He looked me in the eye and said, "We're sorry to bring you this news, but two people believed to be Keith Oaks and Janet Oaks are deceased. Single car accident on the Blue Rock Bridge in Otterton, Ontario."

People came and went through the back door reserved for staffers and deliveries. We stood a few short yards (thankfully, out of earshot) from the comings and goings.

"Accident," I said, focusing on the eyes of the young cop.

"It appears your father lost control of the vehicle, sir. We're sorry." He didn't flinch.

I looked about, people moved around, talking to each other, maybe thinking about things other than what they were talking about, thinking perhaps of tasks to do or what they would do that night.

These two cops, given the sad job of visiting me. How many times would they do this in their lives? We all have our own versions of routine.

My parents were dead. Drove off the bridge. The police were sorry.

I imagined the spiral of the plunging car, turning the way I saw my father turn the wheel, with intent. Off the bridge.

A thousand screaming arguments between my parents, with me captive in the backseat, strapped in. An accident. Was this a mistake? People shuffled past the checkpoint, and the security guard looked away.

My mother, yelling at Dad until he squealed like a tortured animal, begging her to stop. I had thought I'd given up on them, put them behind me, moved into my own life. Dad, snapping at her with bottled rage. The police said nothing more. They looked at me. They were sorry.

Dad, cowering. Mom on a rampage. Dad losing his mind. We go on a picnic. We give our lives...to Jesus, to Slender Nation. They were gone. He lost control. No, he didn't.

"The authorities in Otterton need someone to ID the bodies," the woman said.

"I'll go."

"We'll take you there."

I went to grab my coat. It was no accident, and it wasn't murder, but something in between, something in that space where they'd lived their lives. The last thing I grabbed was my MP3 player. I didn't want to be without music, especially now.

And that's how I left the Royal Ontario Museum in an unmarked police car. We rolled out of the city on the highway while I drowned my senses in the one hundred and thirty beat-per-minute world of trance.

When we stopped, two hours had passed, and my arms were folded together inside my sleeves, right arm up the left sleeve, left arm up the right, my loose straitjacket. The flesh above my elbows was pinched to bruising, pinches on top of the scars of twenty years of pinching and scratching. The woman officer looked at me. "Cold?" she asked.

"No, I'm fine."

We were at a non-descript civic building in downtown Otterton. I was led to a room, and the sheets were drawn back. It was them, undeniably them. I saw only their faces. Dad's nose was flattened, teeth broken and face bruised. Mom's jaw was out of place, eyes askance, her red hair matted with blood. Poking out from the sheet was her button, big and pink, "Ask Me How to Lose Weight!" I unfastened it and put it in my pocket.

Drained of life, they'd become serene. They'd lived fearing death but also looking forward to it, in that strange contradiction of the evangelical.

Admittedly, neither of my parents believed they'd ever really die, especially my father. Since 1981, when I inadvertently led them to a life with Jesus, they'd been expecting The Rapture. They wouldn't die, but would instead fly to heaven intact, leaving everyone else behind. It was supposed to be eternal, but it didn't work out.

I thought of the paradise they had waited for, the afterlife of perfection. Did it matter anymore?

"Yes," I said. "That's them."

After the long drive back to Toronto, I asked the officers to drop me at the museum. I didn't want to go home. They offered twice to stay with me, but I dismissed them with a wave. They wanted to answer whatever questions I might have. They wanted to drive me home.

"Please leave," I said and turned to go, and they rolled on into the Easter weekend, possibly reluctant to let me go, but more likely relieved.

It was well after hours, but I signed myself into work. Suddenly famished, I bought a candy bar from the vending machine, ate it in two bites as I went upstairs to the lab. I worked late in the hope of total exhaustion, so that sleep might come easily when I got home. Not certain how to plan a funeral, I took comfort in the familiar.

I can't work except to be rigorously systematic. I don't read the books I preserve. Many are in languages I'll never know. I analyze the physical structure. Others interpret what it all means. All I do is assemble the pieces and revel in the texture, smell, and presence of paper someone made long ago.

My phone had a message from my boss, who'd seen the accident on the news, and also one from Terry. It was the first I'd heard from her since our breakup. I deleted it without listening.

I tossed Mom's button onto a table. In the quiet of the after-hours museum, the question that loomed all around me was the one I couldn't speak: had I done this to them?

FOUR:

Toronto & Otterton, April 2001—Details went fuzzy for a few days. I know this much: I emailed my supervisor to acknowledge my parents' accident, said I'd be away for a while, that it was a private matter and that I didn't want to talk about it with anyone. I packed a bag and drove to Otterton.

I hid out in my parents' house, mostly in the basement. I hid like a child. I hid like my father. The phone and doorbell rang regularly. I ignored both, taking nourishment from piled-up cases of Slender Nation, ingesting with that chalky pink drink the traces, patterns, and fragments of memory.

Terry called my mobile several times. I finally took one of her calls, fearing she might show up here if I didn't speak to her.

"I saw the news," she said.

"Yeah."

"Anything I can do?"

"Wish there was. There's nothing anybody can do." The call ended quickly.

Truth is, I'd have loved to have seen her right then,

but would that be fair? I had ended our relationship, so the price was mine to pay now that I was hurting. Also, how could I subject her to the Hillsviewites?

I left the house to visit the funeral home to handle the details of coffins, a service, and burial. I did my best to pre-empt questions, telling the morbidly polite man who greeted me: "No visitations. I don't want to see people. Funeral will be at my parents' church."

"Which church, sir?"

"Hillsview Independent Pentecostal. It's what they'd have wanted."

"I see. Who should I contact there?"

"When I was a kid, the pastor was a guy named Haroldson. Couldn't tell you who it is now."

"Let's talk about the service for a few minutes."

"I'd rather not. I'm sure they have a way of handling things like this at Hillsview. The pastor can advise. I don't want to meddle."

"You will deliver the eulogy?"

"I guess so," I said, shuddering at the meekness of my voice.

The arrangements over, I returned to the bungalow at the end of Belting Court. The walls screamed at me. In the basement, I contemplated Mom's cases of product, Dad's desk, the drawers of his filing cabinets, and the couch where he'd spent his nights for the last twenty years.

Around me in the stillness were objects that made up their lives, and before me sat the empty pages that were to become a eulogy. I'd been to very few funerals, a natural function of a solitary life, so I didn't know where to begin. How do you summarize two people's lives with spoken word, lifted off a page? I wrestled with what to say, wrestled with the idea of standing up in the church and saying, "Perhaps it's my fault. You know, I really upset them."

Holed up in the house I'd left in the town I tried to forget, I wished for sweetened memory, but was struck instead by stark fact. My parents were dead, which was shocking, but what hit me hardest was my conviction that the way they died was no accident.

And I was to deliver a speech inside the church I had rejected, to an audience that would not welcome me. I was at a loss to express how I saw my parents, and equally at a loss to conjure and express the warmth that would be expected of a grieving son; I would have liked to have said how my parents did their very best, how they were loving and wise, how they had good hearts. I kept coming up short, but I couldn't say what really happened: coherent memory, like clouds, wouldn't form on command.

I wrote the speech in the only form I could: a statement of facts, better known as half-truth. The speech read like a lengthy obit from the paper. I now see that it was simply what I needed, something I could recite with clear, cold authority.

Half-truth, of course, also equals half-lie. The speech I recited at Hillsview Independent Pentecostal Church:

My name is William Oaks and my parents, Keith and Janet Oaks, died last Thursday, the day before Good Friday, in the waters of the Blue Rock River.

Good morning, family members, friends of my parents, and congregants. It is charitable of you to welcome me back on this sad day to Hillsview Independent Pentecostal. This is a difficult way to return home. Everywhere I am reminded of my parents: Mom's eccentricities, Dad's need to be right in his ways. I keep thinking of the scripture, "Why do you seek the living among the dead?"

You all likely know that their deaths have been deemed an accident by the police, that my father lost control and they fell from the bridge in the car. Perhaps it is fitting that we are in this building, as it was here I once saw my parents submerged in water together, on the day many years ago that we were baptized as a family in the glass tank that sits behind the curtain over there. Pastor Harold-son, you were very gentle as you led us to the water.

Keith William Oaks was born August 21, 1936, the only child to my grandmother Eugenie Oaks, who died in 1965, and my grandfather George Anderson, who according to family lore, died before my father was born. Anderson lived in Otterton only a short while.

Dad was christened at St. Andrew's Presbyterian Church and attended Grosvenor Street Public

School. After graduating from Otterton Collegiate and Vocational Institute in 1954, he attended the University of Western Ontario, where he earned a Bachelor of Science degree. Returning to Otterton, he began work in the Meteorological Office of Environment Canada.

Surprises would upset Dad. Predicting weather was important to him. He worked until his office was closed by cutbacks in 1995.

He was a hard person to get to know.

If you were to have asked my father how life turned out for him, I think he would have taken a long breath and said, "Well, it was okay, I guess, all things considered and other things being equal. There are far worse things that can happen to you. At least we found Jesus."

Dad took solace in the love of God, family history, and prophecy from the Bible.

In 1967 he met Janet Stephen. They married in 1968, and I was born in 1970. After a brief separation from my mother, he joined this church in 1981.

Janet Stephen was born May 15, 1947 in Biscotasing, Ontario, a now near-deserted Northern Ontario railway town, so remote that hydro and reliable road access only became available in the 1980s. Bisco is best known as the 1920s home of Archie Belaney, the Englishman who reinvented himself as Grey Owl, a supposed Indian chief who

*became one of the first modern voices of conserva-
tion. My grandfather John worked as a lumberman
and handyman. My grandmother Frances worked
in the family home. John Stephen died in 1967 and
Frances in 1972. Mom's older brother, Phil, left
home as a boy on a remote-location scholarship to
boarding school in Toronto around the time Mom
was born, returning for summer vacations and
other occasional visits. Mom would cry each time
he left. Often told in our house were her accounts
of Phil boarding the train. Each time, she desperately wanted to go with him. My grandmother
would often be forced to restrain her.*

*Mom attended Biscotasing School, a squat
building next to the graveyard, where the curricu-
lum went to grade eight. She continued on to high
school in Ramsay, Ontario by taking the train each
day, on the schoolcar. She left her hometown at age
sixteen, after completing grade eleven, which was
the highest grade taught in Ramsay.*

*My grandparents bought her a ticket to Sud-
bury and gave her money for her first month's rent.
She was to find a room, a part-time job, and finish
high school. But instead, she indulged her sense of
adventure by staying in Sudbury only a moment,
just long enough to buy another ticket and transfer
trains to continue her travels on toward what she
hoped would be civilization. She eventually found*

her way to Otterton. In time, she would take a secretarial job at Otterton Collegiate, then marriage to my father and motherhood. She wanted to be passionate about everything she did.

Mom often spoke of a recurring dream. It went something like this: "When I dream about Bisco, it's never our house or school or Phil or even my parents. It's always the railway tracks, walking the rails by the lake. It's always sunny and the wind is blowing so there are no bugs, and I smell the pine and spruce—you smell those trees with your lungs, not your nose—and it's sweet and green. In my dream Bisco is beautiful at first, only beautiful, but as soon as I realize how beautiful it is, I know I'm dreaming, and the sun starts going down, but I hang on and hope the good day will stay. I dance around and around by the railroad, and there's a song in my head, and I want to hug the whole world, but I know it's a dream and that it's ending, that it's Bisco and it's a nowhere full of drunks and blackflies and worse—so awful and so beautiful. It gets dark and I can't see. I try to run away up the hill in the darkness, but I don't find the path, and I scream but my voice makes no sound."

The story always ended with her looking at me and saying, "Isn't that funny?"

Though Dad often pushed her to visit Biscotasing, speaking his desire to see "the historic frontier of the north," she steadfastly refused. Dad romanticized her hometown, much as he did all things from the past, but her attitude was more practical. "Biscotasing is a place to be from," was all she would say.

In 1981, Mom joined this church and also began what she called "the enterprise of her life." Many of you know, eat, and sell Slender Nation. For twenty years she credited Slender Nation and her personal relationship with Jesus Christ as the foundation of our family.

Janet Oaks died this past Thursday, killed on impact when my father's car struck the river after driving off the Blue Rock Bridge.

If you want to see them the way I remember them, I have with me a photo that I took on my eleventh birthday.

We join together in sadness today.

Yet, I am not surprised by how they died.

I am not surprised at all.

May they rest in peace.

FIVE:

Toronto, April 2000—I first met Terry a year earlier on the late-night streetcar, coming home from a rave. I was sipping water, keeping to myself, watching out for drunks and also for the looming downer that would soon eat up Sunday morning. It always happened, the music would move me to a high—never needed the drugs that other people took, but even without the drugs, there's always a coming down. The streetcar was nearly empty, but she sat down directly across the aisle. She tented her hands on the seat in front of her and let out a long breath. Her hair was dyed black, and her clothes were faux ragged and scraggly. Her skin looked pale and perfect, and she blew on her hands, and I knew what she was thinking by just looking at her.

"It's a pain, isn't it?" I said.

She stopped blowing and considered her hands, brows knitted. "Yes," she said. She turned to me with eyes both sad and alight. "Yes it is," she said. "Isn't it all a pain?"

"I like that," I said.

She said, "So do I."

We went to a diner that never closes, up on Dupont Street, and ate two breakfasts each. We tried to find uncommon ground but failed, tried to annoy each other but failed. She liked the club music, she liked to be alone, and here we were, two loners keen to be with each other.

"So do you do this every week?" she said, eating an egg-soaked forkful of potato.

"Do what?"

"Pick up on the streetcar?"

I thought about it and said, "No. I've never picked up anyone in my life."

She rolled her eyes and then stopped, the fork twirling in her hand, "My God. You're serious."

"Of course I am."

"Long time since you had a girlfriend?"

"Never had a girlfriend."

"Yeah, right."

"I mean it. What's to lie about?"

"Ever been out with a girl?"

"No."

"You're gay?"

"No."

"You're sure you're not gay?"

"Think so."

"How do you know you're straight?"

"Not sure. I think you look nice. Does that count?"

"When you think about sex, what do you think about?"

"I don't think about it."

She stopped, looked up at the plastic yellow-and-black lettering on the menu. "How old are you?"

"Twenty-nine."

"And you're... Oh, my. You're?"

"Yeah. I've never."

She looked stupefied, and I should have been embarrassed but I wasn't. She made me comfortable. I'd never spoken to anyone this way.

"No way."

"It's true."

"Are you religious?"

It was a hard question. "That's more complicated," I said. "I'm not, but I am. I mean, I was, once." I looked up and down the diner counter—old, chipped beige Formica—populated with a long line of late night stragglers: garbage men and cops sipping coffee, two old cooks, and other nightclub refugees like us filling themselves with grease. Only now did I begin to feel awkward. Publicly discussing my virginity, and possible asexuality, didn't tense me up, but venturing into religion did.

"Sorry, didn't mean to pry," she said, with a hand on my shoulder, and my unease slipped away.

Terry and I walked around and around as the sun came up and the city woke up and we both warded off the downer. In front of an old house on Christie Street, weather worn with four doorbells and six bicycles chained to the porch, she said, "This is my place."

"Nice," I said, to be polite.

"No, it isn't," she said, and I nodded ever so slightly, not enough to be rude, just enough to let her know that I knew what she meant and that it was a moment of politeness neither of us really needed.

Before I could say goodnight and walk away she said, "You can't come in. You can't stay with me today."

"I don't even know you," I said. "I wouldn't know what to do." I hugged her lightly. She looked bewildered, and I didn't know it was because I was not following the end-of-night script. I'd never been in this play before. She looked at me as though I didn't really exist, as though she'd imagined me. I was so charmed by her, yet walked away. Turning back, she was still there. I asked if I could call her. She pulled a pen from her purse and scratched a number on my hand. She had a delicate touch, but I craved for her to drive that pen so hard it would scar me.

I wrestled with calling her. Waited for days. Days of working late. Days of not thinking straight. Days of scratching and pinching. But then I called, and she was home. I asked if she wanted to go out on Saturday.

"Sure," she said, almost casually, "I really didn't think you'd call."

And that Saturday was as easy as the past Saturday. We sat for hours in an old Ukrainian cafeteria/bakery. Terry was smart and funny and sad, strong and vulnerable, the way a person should be, and she didn't seem to find me weird or boring, which astonished me. I asked her as much as we walked Bloor Street, past the flashing glow of Honest Ed's.

"Sure, you're different," she said. "But lots of so-called normal people have stepped in and out of my life already. I can do with different. I might be a bit different too."

"But you're only twenty-five," I said. "I'm older and nobody has come in or out of my life. Nobody at all."

"You are different," she said. "Way different." If she'd said it in any way other than the way she did—a tone both bemused and loving—it would have been cruel. But she was the opposite, everything but mean.

At her place she asked me in. We walked a narrow alley of garbage cans alongside the house and entered a side door to the basement. "Cellar-dwelling," she said, "is the price I pay for solitude." The place was immaculate, if tiny and run down. "I could live upstairs, with sunlight and a view, but I'd have roommates."

"Do you really want me around?"

"I asked you in, didn't I?"

She stepped toward me and pressed her lips against mine. My body jumped forward, while inside I jumped back. "I don't know how to do any of this," I said. "Kissing, making out, sex, I know nothing of it."

"I haven't forgotten that." She began to unbutton my shirt, but I stopped her. She stepped back, but only for a moment. "You are a project," she said. I didn't want her to see my mutilated arms, but I couldn't tell her why. So she went to my pants.

Soon we were both naked except for my shirt and this thing she wore under her top that covered her arms and the back of her shoulders. We did what people do, and it was lovely, and it made me wonder why I'd avoided sex, this act which, in the eyes of my parents' God, now made me one with this girl who was not blind to my weirdness, but didn't see me as weird.

We lay next to each other, sinking into the sheets, the music we both loved playing low, low enough that I could hear her breaths, a dissonant beat softly against the music.

"What's that thing you wear on your arms?" I said.

"It's called a shrug." I shrugged and she nodded.

"Do you ever take it off?"

"Do you ever take your shirt off?"

"Not when there's anyone around."

"Me neither," she said.

"But you've had other lovers."

"Many. I've been naked with a lot of guys. Naked except for my arms. I've got a drawer full of these." She gestured toward the dresser. "If they don't like it, they're always free to leave. You are too, you know. It's a rule I have: we're both here voluntarily. Commitment's fine when it works, but I'm not committed to commitment."

"I get it," I said. Everything she said, everything she did, made sense. That tradition where you're supposed to have sex with every girl in sight and then find a virginal woman? We turned all that on its head. It was perfect and fun.

"You bothered by that?"

"By what?"

"By all the guys I've slept with?

"No. Not at all. What I want to know is has anyone ever seen your arms?"

"Not since I was a child."

"Me either," I said. I sat up on the bed, looked her in the eyes, and unbuttoned my shirt, tossing it to the side. She reached up, teary eyed, and ran her hands slowly, softly, gently, over the mangled flesh of my arms.

Then she pulled that thing off, deposited it on the floor. Up and down, from just above the wrist to well beyond the elbow, were the cross-hatched scars of many methodical knife cuts, a squared-off pattern against unblemished skin.

If it hadn't happened before, it was then that I fell for her. For beauty, for spirit, and because she was the first person I met who did what I did. I was not alone; it was energizing and unnerving.

And, while I'd never sought out sex, I liked it. She had patience; she was a teacher and I her student, and we were both happy. We kept at it. It was intimacy and I was not afraid.

We started seeing each other all the time. I made excuses to not make any trips home and avoided calls from my parents, so that I wouldn't have to lie. Even though I'd long ago stopped believing in their hell, direct dishonesty was repugnant. I embraced the dishonesty of avoidance.

It was six weeks before I asked Terry about her scars, and even then I asked only because she asked me first. We were lying in bed.

"Where do your marks come from?" she said.

"From me, from scratching, pinching, pulling. What about you?"

"From me as well," she said almost indifferently, "from a razor." She ran her fingers through my hair. "I did it a long time ago, was working something out. My home-made tattoo. For a time, that was my art. Cutting lines that nobody can take away. My scars are my own."

I placed my arm against hers, letting our dull skins brush, hardened skin with no sense of touch except for pressure. I grabbed the remote and turned on a CD I'd mixed for her. We melted into the bed, immersed in music and each other, lulled by waves of sound. Her scars were beautiful, and they made mine feel right. I loved her.

SIX:

Otterton, April 2001—"Be comforted in the love of Jesus," said a man as I stepped from the podium at the end of the eulogy. He moved into the aisle and stretched out his arms as if to hug me. "Your parents are eternally reunited with Him in Heaven."

I didn't embrace him, but stopped to think about what he said. "That would not be Heaven," I said. "Furthest thing from it."

"Feel His love," he said.

"Please don't touch me."

"Jesus can forgive, can comfort you."

"Don't touch me."

"Feel His love and know they are together." He wrapped his arms around me, and I could smell his minty breath. I grabbed him by the shoulders and shoved him out of my way, pushing past others who moved to grope me in the name and love of Christ.

"Satan has you in his grasp," yelled another man. He was old, gaunt, skin drawn tight around his bald head, his eyes full of the gleam of judgment. "You must be washed in the blood of the Lamb." I turned away. He lunged, yelling "Sexual deviant, foul spirits come out!" I knew this would happen, but I was not ready.

"Heal him, cast out the devils of perversion!" screamed a woman in my ear. A hand flew up at me. I batted it away and walked on, tunnelling up the aisle.

"Only Jesus can forgive you," said a woman, hunched and thin with hair like a well-kept nest. From somewhere came a shouted Amen.

"For what?" I said, but didn't linger for her response.

Then came the moans, those ubiquitous moans that always seep from the walls and floor at Hillsview. I stood accused, a criminal in the stocks, scourge of the town square.

The funeral—that neat and tidy shroud of a ceremony to remember the dead and commune with the living— the funeral started a familiar caterwauling, familiar though I'd forgotten how intense it would be. Life is fibre and fabric. Strands of life align, mesh, bend, strain and rip, sometimes evenly, sometimes with a jagged edge.

I pushed on, made headway, but in the open space outside the church, a man who looked familiar, an old face from my old life, came at me with a Bible held high as if to hit me with it. I pushed back at him in the centre of his chest and his face went wide eyed and white as he waited for Jesus to restore his balance. A younger, stronger man stepped forward and punched me in the face. We locked arms, wringing and smacking at each other in a twisting dance, the faces around us accusing me. They shouted me down as though I'd been shouting at them, but I had spoken the eulogy with an even voice. They told me I could be forgiven, but none seemed happy about this possibility. Their faces became a blur of sky and concrete. Sounds rose up, and I fell down.

In the end, I let him punch me until he was done.

As we were separated and the hurt rose within me along with the moans and shouted prayers of the Hillsviewites, I saw Pastor Haroldson from afar, in an unfamiliar place behind the crowd. He looked sad and old, a spectator now and not the fiery preacher I remembered from childhood. Still, he was judging me with the rest of them. He didn't speak. He stayed in the back because the crowd carried his damning voice. I broke away toward my car. In the background someone yelled, "You crazies. What are you doing? His parents are dead." I looked back to see Uncle Phil—Mom's only brother, whom I barely knew—shaking a fist at the crowd. I kept going.

The officer who reported on the assault at the church, himself a member of Hillsview Independent Pentecostal, later said to me, "Given the circumstances, we've chosen to not lay any charges against you."

"What about the guy who beat me up?"

"We can't determine who did what."

Mob rule: when everyone is a perp, there are no witnesses. I faulted the police for missing the truth of the assault, but in the end, I couldn't fault them very long for missing the truth of my parents' deaths—blood tests and skid marks grasp only a moment, in this case the final one, and don't show the whole. My parents' lives were a glacial violence whose movements aren't seen in a single glance, can't be captured except to be told.

I won't recant, deny, repent, pander, lie, or lie down. But I'll elaborate, if it kills me. I won't say who was Right or who was Wrong. But I will tell you what I saw.

This is who we were.

PART TWO: NOTES ON A EULOGY

SEVEN: *"Hillsview Independent Pentecostal"*

Otterton, 1981—I first set foot in Hillsview as an eleven-year-old, in the November of Dad's gone-ness. It was me who led our family to Jesus.

I was alone at home, and, finding in the pocket of my jeans a small blue card that asked "Do you know The Answer?" I decided that I should find out. I took three buses across Otterton on a Sunday evening. The card had been given to me by a man at the mall near our house. Mom was out, trying to sell diet drinks and make a fortune. She was new to Slender Nation then, and it hadn't yet shown any results.

I set out for the bus stop in an early winter snowfall. By the time I arrived at the church, I'd travelled beyond all the places I knew, beyond my neighbourhood of squat houses, school, the mall, beyond downtown and its old stone buildings and storybook gabled homes, beyond the neighbourhood that stood beyond downtown, a neighbourhood that mirrored my own with its own mall, its own school, its own squat houses.

Hillsview was a flat-roofed, grey, windowless building on a street of darkened warehouses by the auto plant, surrounded by a parking lot quickly filling with pickup trucks, Chevs, and Pontiacs. Like everywhere in Otterton, Dad's little green Honda would have been out of place. I looked for it just the same; I did this wherever I went since the day he left.

Towering above, instead of a steeple, a broadcast antenna with bright red lights blinked the falling snow pink. A white cross bolted to the steel door made a door handle.

I grabbed the base of the cross. The door swung open easily despite its weight.

A burst of light and sound struck me, magical and happy. People spoke with loud voices, and I was filled with a sense that something incredible would soon happen. The air was musty, sweaty. Not the breezy sweat of a day at the beach, but a heavy mix of people smells, circulated by ceiling fans. The floor of black-and-white tile looked grey and brown with age, but still polished as clean as it could be. Exuberant voices surrounded me: people talking, greeting, hugging, and loving each other. A hand appeared before me. I jumped back.

"Hello, son," said a bespectacled man with greying military hair and gold glasses.

I took another step back. He brought his hands together. "It's nice to see you here."

"It's, uh, it's nice to be here," I said.

"Are you here with your parents tonight?"

"No."

"Friends?"

"No."

"The bus ministry?"

"No," I said, fearing I might be kicked out for not belonging.

"Well, would you like someone to show you around?"

"Uhm, no thanks, I'm fine," I said and instantly regretted it, because he was a good man, and I was glad to have somebody to talk to.

"You sure?" he said. I sucked in a mouthful of air.

"No, actually, yeah. I'd like to be shown around, thank you."

He helped me hang my coat, introduced himself as Mr. Crawford, and brought me to meet Mrs. Crawford. She was big and sturdy like a wall in a green dress, standing with three other women who looked like her. She said hello with a full voice. Together we passed through a pair of steel doors and were greeted by more smiling people. The place had once been a parts warehouse; we'd walked past the order counter, now a vestibule, into the back shop, now a sanctuary. On the floor a crimson carpet pushed back against my feet, making my steps bouncy. The cinderblock walls and the corrugated ceiling glowed white, all painted, painted right down to the conduit that spidered from an electrical panel covered over with the slats of a picket fence. Rows of steel chairs laid out a grid of three sections before a white stage backed with a choir riser and a blood-red curtain. A white cross, brightly lit, glowed in front of the red curtain, suspended by thin wires from the ceiling, a floating mystical apparition. People smiled, waved, shook my hand, and I felt welcomed, loved.

The risers filled with people emerging from behind the curtain: a choir, dressed normally, no robes, no uniforms. A man in a beige suit walked out and stood near the podium. The crowd clapped and cheered. He was a tall, round man with a round face and round glasses.

The choir sang a song that sounded beautiful, and people in the crowd began to sing with them.

Mr. Crawford put a book in front of me, opened midway. "Here's what we're singing."

"I don't know how to sing."

"You don't have to know how, not here." He placed his hand on my shoulder. "Your voice can sing as loud as it wants to go."

I sang and it felt good.

> There is power
> Power
> Wonder working power
> In the blood
> Of the lamb

We sang this over and over, and smiles directed my way filled me up, and something broke loose inside. I was loved, and I loved everyone.

The man in beige was Pastor Haroldson, and after they collected money he began to speak, in a voice that rattled hopeful and angry and pleading and hopeful again. He spoke for a long time, often near tears, and I listened to all he said.

The pastor spoke about how we all belong.

He spoke about how we were united in a great love, greater than all humanity, and how the evil heart of humanity had declared war on us, hating us all the more because of our love.

The pastor spoke of how husbands belonged to wives, wives to husbands, children to parents, parents to children, families to God.

He spoke of the lonely being comforted.

He spoke of broken homes being mended, and I thought he meant falling down houses until I realized it meant us.

He spoke of how there would be no more pain.

He spoke of the power of God to make right the mistakes of history.

He spoke of a golden city, our righteous reward.

He spoke of evil, to which we were all born, of eternal flames if we did not repent.

He spoke of how the flames would burn hotter than any known fire, yet our flesh would not be consumed, and we would not be able to sleep, and it would be outer darkness despite these flames, and it would last forever and ever, and this made me scared.

He spoke about how we don't know when our last chance will be, and I thought about Dad leaving, about how I'd told myself that he'd be back by morning as he pulled away, even though I knew he was really gone this time.

He spoke about how Jesus would soon return to gather his followers. It would happen in the twinkling of an eye. It might happen before he finished the sermon (it didn't, but that didn't change the truth that it could have happened).

He said that it's now or perhaps never.

The pastor spoke of how I must be saved.

And he was right.

The choir sang, "Just as I Am." Though they weren't the best singers, they did their job well: slow and mournful, full of the possibility of hope.

The pastor said come forward if you need to get right with God.

I stepped into the aisle and once again felt the bounce of the crimson carpet. I walked toward the sound of the choir, toward the podium and the pastor, and the world moved slowly.

I arrived and hands were everywhere, waving slowly in the air to the flow of music, hands all over me, on my arms, face, the top of my head, my neck. A gentle hand, pink and smelling of soap, passed before my eyes and rubbed my cheek. A bony hand was firm on my shoulder. A hand rested on my forehead with the oniony scent of a house that hadn't been cleaned. Perfumed hands, calloused hands. Hands and the people laying them surrounded me on all sides, our bodies pressed together in writhing flesh of love and worship. The people touching me prayed, mumbles punctuated with shouts. Incoherent words, in a language I didn't know, sounded from all directions. Some made humble pleas, some joyous, others angry, but all charged with a passion unlike anything I'd ever heard. Nobody explained what they were doing or saying. A big group moan rose up as though drawn directly from me, from inside, from what the pastor called my soul.

Pastor Haroldson stepped from his podium and moved with deliberate grace to where I stood. At first I saw only flashes of beige or the slick top of his head until the crowd in front of me parted and I stood face to face with this man who spoke directly to God.

He pulled a small, clear bottle of oil from his suit. His hair was thin, grey where it wasn't black, and I wondered if the oil was for his hair. He dabbed a few drops onto his finger and traced on my forehead, stared fondly at what he'd written there, and looked up at the ceiling trusses, at lights that shone in blinding fury. He closed his eyes. His arms rose and he silenced the moans, saying, "Praise be to you, Lord. Praise to you that one so young can find you. We thank you for this new life, this glorious soul won over to you from Satan's clutch." He opened his eyes and locked his gaze on me. "Tell us your name son."

"William, William Oaks."

"Who brought you here tonight, William?"

"Nobody," I said. The room went quiet. "I took the bus. Three buses, actually: the eight, the twenty-two, and the seven." Laughter burst out, and I was mad because they were laughing at me but then, was I sinning? Mad at people who wanted to love me? I again feared they'd kick me out, unworthy.

The pastor raised his hands in a quieting motion. In his gaze I saw wholeness, and my anger drained away. "Take my hands, son, as we enter the most holy of prayers." I did. My hands were in his and pressed on my chest, and the group drew in tight around us. "William, I want you to repeat after me." I nodded in a bowing gesture. Oil ran down the bridge of my nose.

"Dear Jesus," went the prayer. "I come to you alone, of my own will. I am sorry for my sins. Thank you for dying on the cross for me. Come into my heart as my personal Lord and Saviour, so that I may be born again. I pledge that the only way to eternal life is through you, that your pure, shed blood was for me, that you would have died even if it was me alone who needed salvation, that I was unworthy until you bought me with your blood, that all other paths except your salvation will lead to damnation. Save my soul and deliver me from my life of sin and eternity in Hell."

Voices of praise again rose throughout the church — from those huddled with me at the altar, and echoing from the rows of chairs behind us and from people standing by the exits. It was not a clatter, but a beautiful random harmony of people thanking the God that made them and saved them: a collective voice shouting, "Hallelujah and Praise the Lord!"

The choir sang softly.

From within rose a happiness, a sense that I was where I was supposed to be. I'd come home to a place that had been waiting for me since before I was born. Energy radiated into and out of my chest, to my toes and up to my head and everywhere in between. I could feel an electric charge, could almost see the sparks that passed between me and the pastor and those around us.

I felt loved. An eleven-year-old boy engulfed in a sweaty burning glow.

"Your parents, let's pray for them," said the pastor. "Where are they tonight?"

"Mom's out selling," I said. "I haven't seen Dad in two months. I don't know where he is, but he's coming back soon."

He became grim. "We'll pray for them now," he said.

He closed his eyes, and so did I. The hands upon me tightened once again, as shouts of "Yes, Lord!" and "Please, Lord!" fired out around me as Pastor Haroldson bellowed, "Jesus, we call on the intervention of your power and grace, purchased by your blood, to make this family whole. To bring this father home. To save his soul. To show this mother the error of her ways. That she may come to know you. Intercede on their behalf, dear Lord, for them and for all who suffer because they don't know you, for all who're lost, for all who've been deceived, whoever and wherever they may be. We claim it in your name that it SHALL be done!"

All around me, people said "Amen" and began to pull away as I was struck by the prospect of my parents going to hell while I went to heaven, that we might never be together again. They would burn forever. Mom must be saved. Dad, wherever he was, must also be saved. They could die anytime. Or Jesus could come back. I had to get them to God, soon.

Mr. Crawford drove me home. The snow turned to slush as we moved across Otterton in his wide black car. Mrs. Crawford tried to speak with me, but I couldn't talk, consumed instead by a lurking fear at the centre of me, growing and churning from behind my ribs.

EIGHT: *"This is a difficult way to return home."*

Otterton, 2001—Uses of calcium carbonate: vitamin supplement, chalkboard chalk, and antacid. It's what papermakers sometimes throw into the pulp to reduce the acidity. Toss a Rolaids into your roll of acid-free paper. I was eating rolls by the dozen.

I stayed in Otterton after the funeral instead of driving back to Toronto. With a puffy face and sore ribs, I drove to my parents' house from the cemetery. Uncle Phil and some of the people from church wanted to come with me, but I begged them not to. I wanted to be alone in the house. I stepped inside the front door and collapsed, doubled over with a horrible burning pain in my stomach that I couldn't master. I left the house, bought a large bottle of antacids, and checked into a motel.

Over the next week, I cleared their home by day, chugging antacids every hour, and stayed in the motel at night. I avoided the neighbours, gave away most of my parents' things to charities, and arranged for the house to be sold once all estate issues were settled. Pastor Haroldson stopped by several times as I worked, but I avoided him by hiding in the basement.

I drove home to Toronto through a blinding rainstorm one week after the funeral, after a final meeting with a realtor and a lawyer. It had been difficult to stay in Otterton as long as I had, and I'd been away from work two weeks.

Travelling with me were the things I couldn't throw away. I had Mom's shiny blender, which I'd purchased for her birthday to help her make Slender Nation smoothies. It was unused, still in the plastic wrap that covered it when it came out of the box. I had a box containing Dad's to-do lists, his Bible, and a collection of his favourite pamphlets about Armageddon, The Rapture, and The End of Days. I had the framed sketch *Milling at Blue Rock, 1862*. I had two photos: the photo of Mom, her parents, and Uncle Phil on the train platform at Biscotasing, and my parents' wedding picture, framed but dusty, black and white on the steps of the Presbyterian Church, retrieved from a corner wall in the dark end of their bedroom hallway.

The only other photo I wanted, the picture of Mom and Dad in the car driving home from the falls on my eleventh birthday, had gone missing in the scrap outside the church after the funeral.

An unreachable pain made its home in my stomach. Acid picked at the back of my throat as I drove. My right hand still hurt from the punching. My face had healed.

I told myself that I should have thrown it all in the garbage, that I was being sentimental bringing these things with me. The debate raged inside as I drove the Queen Elizabeth Highway: throw out all this garbage or cling to the past? Eight-year-old Mom, black and white, scowled at me from the picture sitting on the passenger seat. I chomped another antacid and looked away. If I lost any more weight, I might actually disappear, and maybe that wouldn't be so bad. I turned on the music.

I found music when I left home for university. Music and books weren't allowed in our house unless sanctioned by our church or Slender Nation, so music had never been part of my life. During high school, years when I did nothing but study and plan my escape, I didn't have anything to listen to. The radio was banned by the time I entered grade nine, and instead of making friends and sneaking out and getting to know things like music and movies, I simply gave up on all of it, knowing that my best chance to escape was to become a scholar. I dove into books.

Yes, I had the Bible and, yes, I liked it, but when I broke away I wanted more. I started collecting Bibles wherever I could. Thrift-store Bibles and Bibles being given away by churches. I kept a few intact. The rest I hollowed out and used to smuggle in and out of the house everything I wanted to read. I read history and philosophy and literature, all under the guise of the word of God, and somehow all these books felt connected to God, so I didn't see any lie in it.

So began the curious road that landed me at the ROM. I set myself to being very good at any task in front of me, and by the age of twenty-three I had two degrees, the latter of which was in conservation.

I heard the music as I walked down a Toronto street one evening in first year. The sound had a constant beat that was more vibration than rhythm, and a high melody that sounded like joy. It came from a café, and I walked in and asked what it was. The guy at the counter handed me a CD case, and I walked out of the café staring at it, the music so alive in my head I didn't notice that the real sounds had faded away. I took the case to a record store and found the same CD. I'd never owned one before.

I went to a discount store and bought the cheapest CD player I could find and a pair of headphones. Back in my dorm, I turned on the music and lay on my bed. It was a sound I'd never known I needed. This was trance music, and Toronto would soon be teeming with places where it was being made and heard.

I became the most unlikely clubber, waiting all week to go to old warehouses and lose myself alone in the crowd, immersed in the vibrations, feeling them at the centre of my chest.

I never spoke to anyone. Never tried to. Why would I? All I wanted was the music.

I started acquiring music and sound equipment. Soon I was mixing together stuff on my own. It was the first bliss I'd known since getting saved but, unlike coming to Jesus, this time it stuck.

I get that most social people won't understand how I live—why would they? Social people don't know people like me exist, because we don't talk. But we're everywhere, in every town and every workplace. Guys like me, and women like Terry, it turns out, are even in the nightclubs too.

Music was the final branch in my holy trinity: reading, paper, and music.

Toronto appeared out of the mist along the darkened lake, and I was floating, suddenly stuck between homes. The city I'd called home for more than ten years now looked foreign, its towers and high-rises a pinhole mosaic of light in the gloom.

Without thinking, I skipped the turnoff to my neighbourhood and continued driving, soon finding myself at the back entrance of the Royal Ontario Museum. It was eleven on a Friday night, and apart from security guards and revellers at a late-night event in one of the galleries, the building was deserted, which is how I prefer it.

I signed in with security, grabbed a cart from outside the loading dock, piled in the remains of my parents' things, and went down the hall and up the elevator to my lab. I put everything on a high empty shelf at the back and hung their wedding photo on a nail in the corner. Nobody would notice. I work alone. Even the blender was inconspicuous. I set the photo of Mom and Phil in Biscotasing face down on top of the box of Dad's lists, so that I wouldn't see it as I worked.

The message light was flashing on my phone.

"William, Pastor Albert Haroldson here…" Delete.

"Hi, William, it's your uncle Phil…" Delete.

"Albert Haroldson calling for William Oaks…" Delete.

In total I had five messages from Pastor Haroldson and three from Uncle Phil, as well as one from Jackie, an Egyptologist who worked on the floor above. I returned Jackie's message and made a mental note to screen all calls for the coming weeks. My need to avoid Haroldson was obvious; I wanted nothing from him.

Uncle Phil was more complicated. I would have liked to have wanted to speak with Mom's estranged brother, but couldn't. I felt no malice toward Phil; I simply wanted no further reminders of home than those which I brought with me.

I stepped out onto the walkway bridge that crosses a sky-lit atrium inside the museum. Four stories below, a jazz band played and the last of the partygoers, affable, jovial, standing near the bar, disheveled in their finery, laughed and drank and clinked their glasses and tried to ignore their aloneness.

I went home, relieved by the solitude.

NINE: *"...Dad's need to be right in his ways."*

Otterton, 1981—Rightness was a balm for Dad, a birthright from which he couldn't stray. He shared this need with my mother, along with their propensity for fear. For her, rightness was something to strive for, to cling to. He saw it as inheritance, from which he could not be parted. Rightness was the common ground for their murder-suicide of a marriage. Their union a lattice of fears, fear of nearly everything, married to a requirement to be right.

Abject Fear, do you take Addiction to Rightness, as your loathing spouse? I do. Addiction to Rightness, do you take Abject Fear as your lifelong partner, till driven madly to a soggy grave? I do.

Oaks family history, as told by my father, had it that the great mill at Blue Rock Falls, "in its time the largest in the British Empire," was built and owned by my great-great-grandfather and that by this, because of this, I was important. "You have the same name, William! William Oaks," Dad would say with bright eyes, his hands trembling. The first William Oaks, said Dad, was as generous and trusting as he was wealthy, and because of this he was swindled.

"But he was not stripped of his dignity," Dad said, eyes glazed like a cherub, voice righteous with indignity and reverence. "He chose to repay evil with goodness."

"What happened to him?"

"He died young. I remember the first time Granny told me. I was five."

On my eleventh birthday, in the fall of 1981, a week before Dad vanished, my parents gave me a camera and announced we'd go to Blue Rock Falls. I'd been asking to visit there since I first heard of the place years before. We drove in Dad's little green Honda, descending to the highway by the river on a ramp from the bridge, passing the spot where they would die twenty years later. Dad drove slowly, Mom fidgeted in the passenger seat, and in the tiny backseat I turned the camera over and over in my hands, in near disbelief that this thing gave me the power to stop time.

Many people in Otterton cross the river every day, but I doubt many give it much thought. I thought about the river all the time, not just because it cut our town in two, but also because of the mythical falls.

Upstream, we arrived through hot haze at a gravelly parking lot surrounded by trees, beyond which came the roar of surging water. I concentrated on every last sight, trying to press into memory each overhanging tree branch, every pathway, every discarded bottle cap, each rock. We hiked to a spot above the falls for a picnic. Dad sweat through his shirt carrying the cooler of neatly wrapped sandwiches. Mom looked around in terror at the forest, asking repeatedly about bears. We ate quietly, and after lunch, Dad and I joined a guided tour.

For my father and me, going to the falls was our moment to glory in how wonderful we were, to glory in all the unspecified goodness that William Oaks the First bestowed on us and the world. I was eleven, and in the twilight of childhood's magic, I expected to be greeted with reverence at the falls for who we were, not just by people, but by the waterfall itself.

Dad was forty-four. He expected the same.

In the misty vapour, the round-bellied conservation officer, his uniform green and brown, welcomed us and spoke with a steady voice as he gestured across the surging river. "The indigenous people believed the falls held mystical power."

"The real power," Dad said to me, his voice only slightly hushed and loud enough to interrupt the guide, growing louder with the proud authority of each word, "was mechanical—for the mill. Would have been electrical, too, if William Oaks had lived. The *Indians* were too primitive to know." I drank in Dad's words because they were about William Oaks, so they were about me and Dad couldn't be wrong. But the puffing vanity in my chest came with heaviness. The stories of our once-upon-a-time greatness made me hungry for something I couldn't see.

The tour stopped while the guide waited out Dad's interruption. Annoyed glances stared back at us and I was angry at them for not receiving us as they should, but also at Dad for drawing attention.

"Shh, Dad."

"Don't shush. This is important. This is who you are."

"May we proceed, sir?" said the guide.

"Certainly. I was just filling in some of the mistakes in your story for my son. He's very bright." The guide led us across a pebbly beach.

"From here," he said, "you can see how the falls below us appear out of nowhere, a cliff that would be like the edge of the world to someone approaching on the river above. Explorers from upstream would get a nasty surprise."

A bald man asked if anyone had ever gone over the falls.

I could have slapped my forehead, or his. How could anyone be so dumb? Everybody knew that local track star Ross Marlborough dove the falls last year and swam away safely. And also there was Bulldog Jannsen in 1896—I'd read about him in *The History of Otterton Region*, a book that, officially, I was not supposed to read, let alone enjoy, because Dad said it got the facts wrong about our family; we weren't mentioned in it at all. I'd read it on the sly at the public library, feeling guilty for doing so and indignant about the book's snub, but also mystified by the likes of Jannsen, who went over the falls in a barrel to win a bet. How could people not know this?

"Unfortunately, yes. There are thirty-seven documented cases," said the guide, "and very few survived. The mill at Blue Rock Falls—" Dad's hand gripped my shoulder. I rose tall, ascending to our moment "—of which we can see today only a few minor ruins, opened in 1861 and was owned and built by the region's industrial magnate of the era—" my ears swelled anticipating my name "—John Franklin."

They got it wrong!

"Franklin built the mill, largest in its time in the British Empire, with proceeds from the mercantile trade he'd established several years earlier at Otterton Junction, which is now downtown—"

"That's not true," said Dad with an authority that, to my young ear, had no delusion. But even though Dad's voice puffed me up, I shrunk down as annoyed glares once again turned toward us. Triumph begat dread. We were right, but nobody knew. The guide smiled benignly. Nobody believed in us.

"It's not true," Dad said again. "The mill was built and owned by William Oaks, same name as my son here. He was my great-grandfather. Franklin swindled him."

"Sir, with all due respect, history records—"

"*Your* history is wrong. It's not what I was taught. And if you had any idea about due respect, then you'd know this." Dad's voice rose with whining rage.

"Sir, please, we're—"

"Awash in ignorance!" His face turned several shades of red. I stood with him as if to go to war, but was paralyzed with embarrassment. Inside me growled both the urge to crawl away and the urge to break things and hit people. The guide's disarming smile spurred my rage, while humiliation reduced me to a flat-footed, open-mouthed stare. The word *ancestor* hung before me, a word so mammoth and true that I wanted to grab hold to it, be anchored to its rock, its steadiness.

"William Oaks built the mill," said Dad. In the bemused faces of the crowd, my name seemed suddenly ordinary.

"Perhaps you'd like to lead the tour? I could learn from you," said the guide.

"Oh, no thank you. Please go on."

"Very well. Historians say—"

"Are you going to keep talking about that swindler Franklin?"

"Rest assured, sir, the remainder of our tour will touch only on natural history."

"I'll stay with you," said Dad, "to make sure you get your facts right." He was happy and angry all at once. He could only be happy when stirred to righteous anger. A man wearing a green ball cap smirked at Dad, and in my mind I threw the man, screaming and begging for mercy, into the rushing river, leaving only his ball cap perched on a rock, but as I did so, he turned into Dad, and as he was swept away he said over and over again, "That's not true. That's not what I was taught."

I slunk away to see the water and be alone.

"He's going to talk about science and nature," said Dad. "You like that. Why don't you come along?"

"I already know all that stuff."

He nodded. "You're a smart boy!" My so-called brightness, in which he fervently believed, was yet another thing that made us better than everyone else. I took brightness, my rightness, as my foremost responsibility.

I traced the river upstream, stepping carefully along the stones of the bank, while Dad went on with the group. By the water I lay down. Staring into the white froth, pictures popped into my head: mushroom clouds by the power lines next to our house melted into a classroom where I was singled out for a wrong answer and said back to the teacher, "You're wrong. That's not what I was taught." In pictures like these I found clenched-fist comfort. They were home.

I drowned my senses in the gurgle and roar of the rapids. Teenagers played on the stepping stones in the river's rush, dangerous horseplay under the guise of nonchalance, and I wanted to be exactly like them. Up on the bank, Mom lay in the sun, cocooned in the blinding glare of a reflector sheet with only her face exposed, using the tanning blanket to block every last ray. I laid my head on the surface of rushing water, cool swirls bubbled past my cheek. I plunged my head in and out of the water, transfixed by the transition of sound, of temperature, and of wind to water. I put my head underwater and stayed there. The world was greenness and light and the roar was duller but so loud, and I wanted to be underwater forever and hear this sound.

I looked back to where my mother lay in her silver wrap. My father had joined her; they sat together on the bank, side by side, not touching each other. The shimmering blur of mist from the falls made a small rainbow about them. She smiled, restful. Dad looked happy too. They were at peace, or at least in truce, forgetting how they'd fought that morning, ignoring how they'd surely be screaming at each other on the drive home. They were peacefully at rest, and by the water so was I.

We left the falls and things returned to normal. They *were* at each other all the way home. Dad drove carefully, as usual, below the speed limit, two hands on the wheel, as he started to complain. The guided tour and historical plaques at the falls were inaccurate and insulting. They made no mention of the Oaks family and "our importance in the history of the falls." They got it all wrong.

Mom called him a "prissy, know-it-all-but-knows-nothing idiot." He called her mean, in the whiny pitch of a picked-on schoolchild. She repeated his words back in mockery.

Like a passive dog cornered, he bared his teeth in sudden desperation. "That's it. Janet, that's it! Go ahead. Snarl at me! Snarl! Snarl! Snaaaarl!" With each snarl he grew louder, drove faster, and swerved the car. His perfect driving broke into sweeping arcs that crossed two lanes.

She smirked at me in the backseat and rolled her eyes. I snapped my first picture, the flash nearly driving Dad off the road. She yelled at him for driving like a maniac. He slowed, straightened, and said nothing more.

It was the beginning of two things I wouldn't recognize for many years: Dad's breakdown, and my realization it was strange that my father needed two weeks' notice, a fully detailed plan, schedule, and itinerary for a picnic trip of less than four hours. He had to know everything that would happen, otherwise he couldn't go. There was no room in his world for things that might happen or for the unknown; only what could be predicted, known, measured, and seen was allowed. It was all one big checklist, and deviations from the list were a weight he couldn't bear.

Mom would say, with predictable regularity, "Knowing what I know now, I would've never married your father. You and I would have done much better with someone else. There are other men out there, real men."

But that day, at the falls, for a brief moment I had seen Keith and Janet Oaks happy. The passage of that moment, like the shadow of a cloud as it briefly obscures the sun, didn't bring lasting comfort. How sad we were.

TEN: *"... the living among the dead."*

Toronto, April 2001—I spent all weekend back in the lab, taking solace in the work, catching up on projects I had dropped during my two-week absence. I re-glued five bindings, tested eight more books, and began the long, slow process of restoring a seventeenth-century map. The key thing to know about books and acid content is a simple date: 1861. Pulp papermaking was mechanized that year. Paper became cheap and easy, spruce forests disappeared, and the resulting books are full of enough acid to keep guys like me working for the next hundred years. My lab has all the chemicals and tools for testing acid content. I use these, but I always start by sniffing the paper and checking the print date.

The weekend was calming, but I chewed away on medications just the same. All weekend I considered the appropriate ways to dispose of the final artifacts of my parents' lives.

I hadn't always been alone. When I was a boy I had friends—the other boys and girls on my street. We played the games neighbourhood kids play. I walked out the door one day, and children were outside, and next I knew we were playing hide and seek. They had to show me how to play, and it was fun, but after a few games I left and went home. Didn't say goodbye to anyone, wasn't called home by my parents. It just never occurred to me that the games could go on.

That joyful, mad craving for endless adventure that children cling to and adults mourn, I never had it. And the crazier, darker wild world of children was one I knew only on my own, in my own thoughts and daydreams: visions of flying above the trees or living beneath the sea, nightmares of being buried alive or going off to war. These were never with a team or a platoon. In my visions, I was alone.

I didn't know that it was unusual to have no close friends.

Yet, up until the break that happened when I was twelve, my dive underground, the games and friendships continued with neighbourhood kids and those I met at school. I liked to run and horse around, but as far as I knew, these people ceased to exist when I could no longer see them. I was never intentionally mean to anyone, couldn't stand the thought of meanness, but nobody else seemed entirely real, perhaps because I wasn't sure if I was real.

And even these light friendships became unbearable when we got saved. Everything was too complicated because I was commanded to witness about Jesus with everyone I spoke to, so I spoke to nobody.

I went through high school the quiet kid with perfect marks, who ducked conversations and always had a reason to be somewhere else. I would get away from here, I reminded myself. I didn't know how, but I knew that school would somehow hold the key.

I went to church each week with my parents and said and did everything I was supposed to, even though the place had become disconcerting, revolting.

And when I got to university, I could work full time on my studies. Yet this never felt like freedom, so I studied all the more, and that got me here.

On Monday, it was like I'd never been away. Everyone surely knew what had happened, but thankfully nobody spoke of it. Discussions of my parents started and ended with a group-signed card from people on my floor and curators I worked with. At 8:47 a.m., my lab was invaded by Jackie the Egyptologist and a big burly grad student, a large man with a boy's face, holding an antique cookie tin in his mitt-like hands.

"This is Bob," said Jackie, exuding confidence and panache, as usual. "He found something in the collection." Bob lifted the lid on the tin and tilted it forward with trembling hands for me to look.

Inside were fragments, some small, some large, but all with a distinctive yellow-and-brown grid pattern. I put on my cotton gloves and extracted a piece. The fray pattern on the torn edge confirmed my suspicion. The fragment, no bigger than my index and middle fingers combined, bore hieroglyphs and part of an image made with several different inks and also what looked to be well-preserved gold leaf.

I could tell it was papyrus by the rounded edges at top and bottom, the straight edges of the lateral breaks, matching the up-down direction in which the fibres had been laid, but mostly I knew it was papyrus by the fact it came into my lab with an Egyptologist and her grad student.

Jackie pulled the fragment from my hand, pinching it between thumb and forefinger. *Bare* thumb and forefinger. I could have thrown up. She was doing it to get under my skin.

"Glad you're back. Guess what we have here?" she said, tapping the cookie tin.

"Cookies?"

"Book of the Dead." Her hand shot to her mouth. "Gosh, sorry, I didn't think."

"Don't worry about it, Jackie," I said. "Sometimes not thinking is the best way, and I'm not offended. What's the project? Let's get started."

She looked relieved and said, "I think it's the rest of the fragment that's been on display out there since the forties. Bob found it in the back of the sixth-floor collection room." He swelled at her words. This is what archaeology has come to: we make our discoveries in our own collections, there being none left to make in a world which offers nothing but pilfered tombs and the bore holes we leave behind. She dropped the fragment into the tin, and I closed the lid.

"It's in good shape," I said.

"Just giving you the heads up," she said. "I'm asking for fast-track approval on the restoration, and when it's granted it'll be you. A lot of people are interested in this."

As she spoke, I stared at the boxes above her holding my parents' memorabilia, perched precariously under a sprinkler head.

My office, my lab, is a funny place. I conserve and restore paper, yet next to my desk is a shredder. The humidity in the room is perfectly controlled with an expensive monitoring system and a gasket-like seal on the door, yet overhead are the ready, able jets linked to the fire alarm. The sprinklers and the shredder remind me of my father. I don't smoke, but I keep a zippo on the shelf. Dad and Mom both believed that you can't be too careful.

But you can. You really can be too careful.

A lot of people would be interested. Exactly what I didn't need. Or maybe I did, a project to keep me busy.

The Book of the Dead. A map for the spirits in the afterworld. If the map led the spirits to the storage and conservation area of the ROM, a thousand pardons to the spirits, but perhaps they'd appreciate the air conditioning. Perhaps they might enjoy the company of my parents' artifacts. When you consider the age of the universe, deceased two weeks is almost the same as dead four thousand years. And if all these spirits were here, perhaps they'd comingle as they watched me work. If they did, would they see it as the afterlife they had hoped for?

It was all just paper. Beautiful glorious paper, flowing translucence, lightness and edge, the plane around which I've built my life. Just paper.

ELEVEN: *"…my father lost control…"*

Otterton, 1981 and earlier; Toronto, 2001—Dad left the day my mother got her big pink button, the one that said "Ask Me How to Lose Weight!"

It started with a fight on a Saturday morning. I heard them yelling from where I sat on the grass, down by the curb. From inside the house, she talked louder and louder until she was yelling. "I don't see what's so wrong," she said. "Why do I have to be stuck in a life where—"

Staring at my shoe, I twisted my foot into a small pile of pine needles. I could never tell who was right when they fought. Usually Dad *seemed* right, but when he wasn't there, she would be right and him wrong.

Another yell came from the house: a squeal, desperate and animal, from Dad.

I crept around the side of the house and back up through the bushes beneath the living room window.

"We need to do this. This is our chance. We'll make a fortune," said Mom.

"We don't need more money."

"Is this house a mansion? Is that tiny car of yours a Cadillac? I'm not getting left behind while the world gets rich."

"But couldn't we—"

"You know what the best time was to get rich? The Great Depression. Smart people bought the land nobody wanted. I'm not missing out. You'd know if you'd grown up with nothing. I've had enough of that."

"We're not *in* a depression, Janet."

"You never know when. Not me. I'm not going backwards, and I'm not missing a chance to get ahead. Why are you always against me?"

"There's risks. Have you looked at—"

"There are NO risks. It says so right here." I heard the shuffle of paper.

"We don't need to get into—"

"We don't. We don't. We don't. I'm married to the king of don't. You're some big thinker, and what do you do? You push paper around a desk at the weather office. I've got a chance at something, and you act like I'm crazy."

It went on. I slunk away to the field near the power lines beside our house. Stepping from our mowed lawn to the tall brown grass, I was in my own world at the bottom of the dead end of Belting Court. The front door flew open and Dad walked out, holding his hands as though raising them to his ears but stopping a few inches short. His face was red. He disappeared around the side of the house, his bare legs a white glow in the sunlight.

I walked to where he'd gone. He sat cross-legged on the concrete walkway next to our carport. He stared at the house next door and the row of low green bushes around it.

He noticed me and said, "Hey, hey there, William." His eyes were glassy and tinged with red at the corners. He ran a fidgety hand along the side of his head. "Hey," he said with an unconvincing smile. "If you look closely at these bushes, there's a chipmunk who's been running in and out. I think he's got a nest nearby." I tried to look interested in the bush. "When you watch them run and leap, it's like they're on a roller coaster." He picked up a leaf, looked at it, then turned to me and said, "You know what? We should go for a ride on a roller coaster today."

"That'd be good," I said. "Really good." I had jumped up without even noticing.

"Then we'll go today—in half an hour—after your mother's gone."

"Where's she going?"

"A renewal rally."

"A what?"

"It's a bunch of people. Listen, your mother might be sad if she knows we're going without her, so let's keep this secret, okay?"

"Okay," I said, not sure if it was. "What're we gonna do until then?"

He took a long breath. "I think I'll just sit here. Sit and relax."

I had a bruise on my arm, about the size of a quarter, from falling down in a game of tag. I pressed on it, feeling the pain rise with the pressure and then recede as I took my thumb away. I did this several times until Dad opened his eyes and said, "Don't do that. That's an injury. Leave it alone."

"Injury" sounded important. I walked inside, pressing lightly again on the bruise after I was around the corner. Mom was putting on makeup and looking closely at her face in the bathroom mirror, stretching her skin, examining with a wide eye. She noticed me standing in the doorway, seeing my reflection in the mirror.

"Now don't be like that, Billy," she said, her tongue pushing her cheek out to apply makeup. "You look like a ghost kid from the railroad tracks. It's no big deal, everybody argues. You have to remember that I have a huge burden in this house." She paused midway through a brushstroke of her red hair and leaned in close to the mirror. "I have to be the man and the woman in our household, and that's a lot of work.

"Your father doesn't understand things the way I do. He thinks he can just go to his job each day and everything will be great. Now, what good is that?" Her eyes met mine again. I shrugged. "Exactly. He has no dreams. And dreams are what make us alive, William!" She dabbed her cheek with cream, ran a finger along her eyebrow. "You can always see the truth in other people by the way they treat money. It's how to see their soul." She searched the counter for pins to put in her hair.

I didn't say anything, didn't know what a soul was.

"Your father won't ever do anything with himself." Our eyes met again, she stopped working her hair. "Don't be like that," she said.

"Okay," I said. "But Dad does things. Downstairs. He sometimes helps me build models."

She frowned and placed her hand on my shoulder. "Models are make-believe, Billy. They're not real. You want to be a doer. What good ever came of a model?" She turned back to the mirror to inspect her face one last time. "I keep this house together, I swear." I pictured her gluing pieces of siding and shingles. "That man. You know your father wasn't the man I wanted to marry?" She was staring into the mirror like it was outer space. "I always wanted to marry an Oriental man. They say that children who come from *mixed* marriages are smarter because of mixing the genes." I saw a large pile of denim pants. "Mm-hmm, mixing genes. And Chinese people are the smartest in the world. It's a fact. And great musicians. So if I'd married one, you'd be even brighter and good at music," she said, smiling at me then catching her own reflection in the mirror, beaming. She touched her nose gently and applied more powder. "Wouldn't that have been wonderful?"

I nodded, but wasn't sure.

"Never managed to get one interested, though," she said, "so, by the time I turned twenty-one I wasn't about to let anyone call me a hippie women's libber or an old maid. I met your father and figured it was time to get on with things. Goodness. Look at that." She grabbed my arm and examined the bruise, poking hard at it. "I wonder if this needs to be lanced. We'd better keep an eye on it." A car honked outside. "That's my lift!" She straightened her skirt. Patting me on top of the head, she ran down the hall and then slowed to a steady and deliberate walk as she turned the corner to approach the door. Through my parents' bedroom window, I saw the woman who was picking Mom up. She had long hair that made her head look big; she drove a small blue station wagon.

After they pulled away, I went to the bathroom and put my fingers to the sides of my eyes and pulled them back. I looked at myself in the mirror with my Chinese eyes. I opened my mouth as though singing. A half-Chinese rock star.

Dad, when I returned to him, wasn't moving, hardly breathing, his eyes shut.

"Mom's gone," I said.

"Let's go."

Soon we were driving. "This is a great day," he said. "This is exciting. We're going to have fun." But he didn't sound excited. We took the ramp down to the expressway. Descending into the ravine, the whole world rose up on either side of us—on one side the familiar mall, gas stations, and restaurants, to the other, downtown with its big old houses and stone churches along St. Andrew's Street.

"Dad, are we poor?" I said.

"No." We drove the rest of the way in silence. I worried he was mad at me. I'd never been to Adventureland, the amusement park, and didn't want to blow this chance.

When we arrived and walked through the turnstile, I ran toward the roller coaster, but Dad grabbed my shoulder and said, "Let's be patient, William." I wanted to pull him this way and that, go running from ride to ride, but he was firm, so I followed along with him, ready to burst. We toured the grounds for an eternity, past rides, concessions, arcades, bingo halls, and bathrooms until finally he said, "Well, now that we've seen everything, we should go on some rides." We rode the Polar Express, the Ferris wheel, the haunted house, and then were on to the roller coaster where we climbed, spun, curved, and dropped. I yelled the whole time, my hands in the air. Next to me, Dad was motionless, hands lightly gripping the bar, eyes closed. The ride ended too soon. "Let's have one more before we go home," he said, perhaps sensing my disappointment.

I picked the bumper cars. It had the longest lineup so it had to be worth the wait. When we reached the front of the line, the attendant said, "Together?" and Dad said yes, and next I knew we were jammed into the same bumper car, him on the wheel, me wedged against the car's metal wall. I wouldn't get to drive. He turned to me and said, "William, promise me one thing."

"What?"

"Don't become like your mother."

"Okay," I said, looking up at him, then dropping my eyes to stare at our legs, side by side on the black ripped vinyl seat. I had lied, but to whom? The lie sank into me, a weight on the centre of my chest.

The bell rang and the cars burst to life. All around us cars banged into each other, the air filled with laughs and shouts and the ozone smell from the whir of twenty electric motors. Two kids could not drive at all and were stuck spinning in circles while others launched at them from all directions.

My father drove with two hands on the wheel, checking over his shoulder before veering right or left, speeding up and slowing down cleanly and smoothly. We did at least seven trips around the enclosure. The bell rang and the ride was over.

"We didn't hit anybody," I said.

"I know," he said. "Pretty good driving, eh?"

He led me out of the ride to a concession stand for a treat. I tried to make the cotton candy last all the way home.

We came home to Mom's pink button and an array of brochures. They fought again, louder and longer than ever. Late that night, I heard Dad's car start, and in the morning he was gone.

Dad kept control in minute ways. He kept a mileage log that documented every transaction in his car, a yellow notebook detailed in tiny, perfect script: Odometer

Reading/Mileage since last fill up, price/litre, number of litres, Total price.

He sought control by predicting the weather, which made his relationship to the weather different from everyone else. Bad weather never got him down if he'd predicted it, and good weather was a nagging nightmare for him if he hadn't said it would happen.

And shopping. He once bought five hundred cans of frozen grape juice because they were on sale. "Just think, William, enough to last until you're in high school!" And as the frosted condensation on the cans melted in the glowing light of the open freezer in our basement, he painstakingly labelled each one with a grease marker: "09/10/79 $.10/$.10" Translation: Purchase Date, Purchase Price, Amount Saved.

I watched, awed by his precision, scared to get too close; I might distract him, might provoke him. You didn't want to interrupt when he was thinking or working, he could explode.

Mom threw all the cans out when we joined Slender Nation. After all, anything but Slender Nation was a Food Crime, it said so, it said it right there, right there in the company pamphlet. I didn't mind so much. That cheap grape juice was awful.

His lists. Thinking about all the things to do, and thinking about thinking about all the things to do. Dad would sit at his desk in the basement every night, five feet from where I was building model airplanes. He would stare at a notepad. Occasionally he'd cross something out, add something new, erase something else, all in his perfect, tiny script, which resembled Helvetica, 4 point. But most of the time he just stared at what was written. If I glanced over for too long, or if Mom opened the door at the top of the stairs, he covered the pad with a blank sheet. When he was done each night, long after I was in bed, he locked the papers away.

I thought he was planning a bomb shelter, and we'd soon have a second home buried in the backyard, lead lined and sealed off to the world, the ultimate playhouse. I mentioned this at school and people called me weird, and it suddenly didn't seem cool anymore. I stopped talking for fear of being left off the kickball team, but also for fear of actually being weird.

After Dad left, the basement of our house became solely mine, apart from boxes of Slender Nation supplies and Dad's clothes and books in lopsided stacked boxes that Mom piled under the stairs.

I made a fort around my desk, in the corner away from the stairs. I darkened it to the outside world by closing a plastic curtain on the high narrow window above. The fort was square, bordered by the corner walls of the basement and two sets of shelves that blocked my view of Dad's empty desk. A musty green shag that had once been in the living room carpeted the cold cement floor. I had strung an extension cord along the ceiling, standing on a swaying chair, to hang a work lamp in the fort, so I could see by the light of its bare bulb.

Inside the fort, shelves were stacked with airplane models and handbooks on model building. Later it would be home for my chemistry set, my introduction to the basic science of my profession.

I left the bottom shelf on one side of the fort half-empty, making a space just large enough for me to crawl through, and this was the doorway. On the wall was the ink sketch *Milling at Blue Rock, 1862*, showing men up high above the falls, skipping across booms with long staffs in hand while the mill's big wheel spun furiously with water delivered by the flume. In the foreground, women in big hats and puffy dresses looked on from the river-bank far below while children played. I secretly retrieved this sketch from the garbage after Mom replaced it with a Slender Nation poster of a sunrise and the words *Wealth through Health*.

I rushed to the fort after school each day, came up only for dinner, and returned there immediately after mixing and drinking my shake.

One night I crept out of the fort and broke open Dad's drawer. It was one month after he'd left. I worked quietly because of the Slender Nation renewal rally happening upstairs. I picked the lock with a paper clip and an awl. There, I first saw the details of his to-do lists, stacks of them, perfectly ordered stacks with hospital corners, not a day missing all the way back to the day in 1952 when, presumably, he began to archive.

The days were nearly identical from one to the next. Only over months and years did they change, so slightly, so slowly, that change was barely noticeable except to fan the pages quickly and see subtle animated shifts in the patterns of words and numbers, like the backdrop in an old cartoon. From one day to the next every consonant and vowel was in nearly the same spot, every item number perfectly placed as the day before. Each day the same things were crossed off and the same things circled.

It's no surprise that every day was the same. Life changes slowly. What amazed me was the repetition of precision. Here is one list:

> May 17, 1961
> 1. Get up early this time (don't sleep in!)
> 2. Stretch, breathe
> 3. Check barometer
> 4. Calisthenics in yard before breakfast
> 5. Breakfast
> 6. Pack lunch
> 7. Get dressed and leave for work by 8:25
> 8. Work
> 9. Go for walk at lunch
> 10. Work in the afternoon
> 11. Leave work at 4:45
> 12. Drive home
> 13. Read newspaper

14. Dinner with mother
15. Relax with mother
16. Read more newspaper
17. Review flyers
18. Plan shopping
19. Check forecast
20. Make plans for tomorrow
21. Get to bed before midnight
22. Sleep better by getting everything done right this time

And here is another:

October 24, 1971
1. Get up early this time (don't sleep in!)
2. Stretch, breathe
3. Check barometer
4. See William before breakfast
5. Breakfast
6. Pack lunch
7. Get dressed and leave for work by 8:25
8. Work
9. Go for walk at lunch
10. Work in the afternoon
11. Leave work at 4:45
12. Drive home
13. Read newspaper
14. Dinner with Janet and William

15. Read more newspaper
16. Review flyers
17. Plan shopping
18. Check forecast
19. Make plans for tomorrow
20. Get to bed before midnight
21. Sleep better by getting everything done right this time

Ten years later, still trying to not sleep in and not stay up late. Weekend lists were a little different from weekdays, but all the Saturdays and all the Sundays were the same.

Three months before I was born this item appeared: "Paint room for baby!" This stayed on the daily list for a good stretch. Mom ended up painting my room herself, eight months pregnant; I know this because she mentioned it to him at least once a week.

Four days before I was born he wrote "1a. Prepare to leave work if labour (Remind Barry about this—he needs to know you may be away from the desk!!)." The day after I was born a new item appeared, "Register Baby William!!" which stayed around for fifteen days, its disappearance matching up perfectly with the registration date on my birth certificate.

The period before and after my parents' wedding showed a few slight blips—"Buy suit"—and for eighteen days "Book honeymoon!!" appeared. This progressed to three exclamation marks, then four, and then disappeared days before the wedding.

No honeymoon happened. Mom often reminded Dad of this as well. She tried to make like it was a joke, "Heck, what's with everybody's big expectations of life? Look at me, I never even got a honeymoon."

A quick glance at Dad's lists might make it seem he wouldn't have tied his shoes or chewed his food except that these tasks were on a list, but the sense I got looking at the lists after they were dead was that he feared that if each and every day was not rigidly defined, then perhaps the day would not happen.

For their final day, there was no list.

In my lab, these papers were my record of him, his existence beyond memory, their volume thicker with the addition of twenty years, their decay more advanced than before, their ink more faded, their words and numbers the same as ever. But in 1981, standing in the musty greyness of our basement that night, picking a lock as Mom practiced sales pitches in the living room above my head, I rubbed the lists, looked closely for hidden messages, held one lightly over a candle to check for invisible ink. The papers were my connection to my father's voice, and I feared my viewing of his sacred papers would prevent his return and that wherever he was he somehow knew what I was doing and I had broken his heart.

My father, my vanished gatekeeper to the mysterious world of being a man, apparently spent every night fretting over, combing, correcting, and changing these papers to produce exactly the same thing while I sat next to him putting together my models of Mustangs and Messerschmitts. How could the adult world—the world of having money and driving cars—be so drab? I didn't see anything else hidden and waiting for me to decode. I didn't see my father's lonely and fretful life in the paper and ink or the smell of mold in the deteriorating fibres. Back then, the mystery of the lists was the absence of the mysterious.

I replaced the lists in perfect order, fretting, as I would for months, about how to fix the lock. When Dad returned he began sleeping in the basement each night on a couch pushed up against the cinder block wall next to his desk, shrouded by curtains. He replaced the lock with one much larger. He kept making lists each night, but said nothing about the lock.

I sketched bomb shelters.

In the lists, Dad's later years seemed more peaceful, more items were checked off, tasks assigned to him at church. "Daily Bible Reading—see notes" or "Set alarm early—Men's Breakfast at Church."

Church gave him human contact and the sense of something larger, which he so badly needed, along with a theology that made life predictable. He crossed off more items than he circled, and this would have pleased him as he made the new list for the following day.

TWELVE: *"... we were baptized as a family..."*

Otterton, late 1981—On a Sunday soon after our family became 100 percent saved (in our case, Dad was the last to find Jesus), a large aquarium-like tank was rolled to the front of the sanctuary.

Wearing white robes that stunk of chlorine, Dad, Mom, and I climbed a rolling staircase to a scaffold next to the tank. There, Pastor Haroldson greeted us. One by one, he led us by the hand to jump over the edge after saying a short but loud prayer.

Dad went first, falling arrow straight to the bottom then rising straight up with a jubilant face. He shuffled aside to make room for Mom. Her arms flew out to her sides as she jumped, her robe puffing full of air and then water.

Just before I jumped, Pastor Haroldson whispered in my ear, "Go all the way under. It won't *take* unless you're covered, right over the top of your head."

I leapt in, felt the soaking coolness, and stayed crouched at the bottom of the tank. It was a peaceful space of shimmery light. The water filled my ears, melding the applause and shouts of the congregation into a loud gurgling murmur. When I came up for air, Pastor Haroldson bellowed, "Behold, a new family in the House of the Lord, washed white as snow."

They cheered and clapped all the more. I touched the top of my head to make certain it was wet. Our robes had ridden high up around us in the water. Thankfully, the front pane of glass, which faced the sanctuary, was heavily frosted.

THIRTEEN: *"... my grandfather George Anderson, who according to family lore, died before my father was born."*

Otterton & Toronto, 1930s–1990s—Here's what really happened: George Anderson met Eugenie Oaks as a newly landed Englishman in genteel Otterton. He was a man of good breeding, he assured her. He was of an old-order family, well established, and royally connected. And how opportune it was, on his travels, his sojourn about the empire, to meet a fine lady of such excellent breeding as herself, a descendant of Otterton aristocracy!

He believed himself.

She believed him too.

They soon married, conceived my father, and within six weeks George disappeared into the night, later arrested in Toronto for desecrating a church. He put a brick through one of the stained-glass windows at Metropolitan United on Queen Street East. It was alleged that at the time of his arrest, he thrashed about madly and shouted about the coming of the answer, that he was here, that he was here, that he was here now, that all would be made good.

His records show that he chattered incessantly to the officers, to other inmates at the Don Jail, and to examining physicians. He stated his royal lineage, warned of the looming apocalypse and the need for his rightful restoration. The growing crisis in Europe could not be ignored. Events called for his return. The world needed answers, and how he would provide for all their needs if only they would listen. He was the lost prince. He was royalty, and you can't imprison a royal!

My grandmother defended him religiously in letters to physicians and lawyers, the superintendent of the Toronto Hospital for the Insane, and the warden of the Don Jail. She pleaded his case: Did they not know who this man was?!

She campaigned then stopped abruptly, writing only one final letter, addressed to both the warden of the Don Jail and the Solicitor General of Ontario:

Dear Sirs,

George Anderson is a fraud.

It has come to my attention that he is neither royalty nor English. I would state that only God knows who he is, except I believe that perhaps even God does not care for this man. My marriage to him is a sham and shall be annulled. You should hang him.

Yours sincerely,

Eugenie Oaks

They did not hang him. He was only in jail because no space yet existed for him in the Toronto Hospital for the Insane, to which the courts had committed him. A hanging did happen while he was in the jail. The condemned man, a rapist named Harry O'Donnell, walked past my grandfather's cell on his way to the execution room, a shaft on the north face of the building where the condemned would fall from the second floor to the first wearing a noose. In face of the quiet, deferential respect inmates showed towards the man on his final walk—respect even for a rapist—my grandfather instead stood at the caged door of his cell and called out to O'Donnell, "You shall be delivered because you walk with me!"

This was enough to get George Anderson transferred out of the jail, perhaps for his own protection. There still being no room at the Toronto Hospital for the Insane, he was moved instead to Ontario Hospital, New Toronto, which was better known by its previous name, Mimico Lunatic Asylum, on the shores of Lake Ontario in farmland beyond the western boundary of the city.

There he began a lengthy regimen of psychiatric care: fresh air, exercise, chapel, and in 1937 he was deemed suitable for a treatment being tried for the first time in

Canada, a medical revolution that would fix everything: insulin shock therapy. Later, he was also administered several new drugs, including nicotinic acid. He was never visited by the wife who disowned him. He was never known by his son.

He was, according to his file, well liked by other patients and the asylum staff. He infused his ramblings with confident articulation. He carried himself well, was well groomed, and walked the grounds with an astute carriage. When I think of him, I see other patients mistaking him for a doctor or a minster, and perhaps he himself made the same mistake. His file also states he very much enjoyed the weekly dances held in the community hall on Saturday nights. While the asylum was a good fit for him, it appears that no progress was made on his delusions. These stayed to the end, coming and going in their severity and their focus, but staying with him nonetheless, like a family member or an old friend.

He died in the asylum in 1951, when my father was sixteen. George Anderson is buried in an abandoned graveyard once owned by the hospital. It sits in the shadow of a freeway, surrounded by industrial yards, in present day Etobicoke, Ontario. His death record indicates "institutional burial."

My father never met George Anderson. My father never believed his father lived beyond 1936. I have stood in the yard where my grandfather was buried in 1951, and I've seen the record of his death.

I'd moved away and was living in Toronto before I began to wonder about George Anderson. He'd always been an obscure footnote in the family history. The absence of his story—where he came from, what he looked like, where his grave was, or how he died—made him stand out from all the others for whom Dad could recite the pertinent facts.

One day on a visit home, under the guise of needing it for a passport application, I asked Dad for a copy of his birth certificate. He granted this begrudgingly. "Why do they need such a thing?"

"It's the government, Dad. They try to take everything." While this was my own made-up nonsense, he didn't investigate any further and produced an old card from beneath his stacks of lists.

"Not sure why you want a passport, son. I've never had one. The world is perilous. Have you watched the news? Evil is on the move out there. Health insurance. You've got to buy health insurance if you go."

The official family story: while my grandmother was pregnant with my father, my grandfather took ill and died. Strangely, this was the only ancestor Dad wouldn't speak of.

For Dad, a single mom was unacceptable, but a widow was tragically heroic. At Hillsview there were many women who showed up each week with children but no father. These would be a focal point for Dad. "Let's hope," he'd say, "that the father is dead, or else the child is surely a bastard."

Luckily, his own mother was just what he wished for: tragically widowed when pregnant one month.

"You're one of the Oaks men," he'd often say, "just like your own father." I was left to figure out what this meant. For a time, trees became venerable. I was sure I could speak with them. But my father's father was not one of the Oaks men.

The path to finding the facts of my grandfather's life was shockingly simple and lucky. I began looking in the microfilmed archives of the *Otterton Record* for his obituary, scouring the months leading up to my father's birth.

I found none.

What I found instead:

LOCAL MAN ARRESTED IN TORONTO

Outrage in Hogtown as George Anderson, of Otterton, was jailed Thursday for a grievous act of vandalism against a sacred building. Anderson, twenty-seven, was arrested on the grounds of Metropolitan United Church, at Queen Street East and Church Street, by patrolling constables who witnessed him throw a brick through one of the majestic stained-glass windows of the venerable building. Anderson is charged with grievous public mischief for this desecration and is scheduled to appear in court

on Monday to answer for his actions, which
can only be seen as another sign of the growing
degradation of society.

And that was all I found in the *Otterton Record*. My
grandfather had made the news! Burning with the desire
to show this to my father, I drove from Otterton Public
Library to their house. We had shakes for dinner, with a
special treat of hot dogs. Hot dogs, as it turns out, were
not a Food Crime if accompanied by Slender Nation (by
then it was decreed that virtually all foods became healthy
and nutritious when ingested with Slender Nation). The
printout of the 1930s crime blotter burned in my pocket,
in my mind, on the tip of my tongue, as the three of us
ate silently together. I had an urge to tell Dad, but I knew
it would hurt him so I let it burn on, keeping it to myself.
I drove home after dinner, and the next day continued
my search at Toronto's brick and glass reference library
on Yonge Street.

The *Toronto Telegram*, February 10, 1936, yielded this
nugget:

CHURCH ATTACKER COMMITTED INSANE.

George Anderson, lately of Otterton, has been
judicially committed to Toronto Hospital for
the Insane as a result of his arrest for violently

desecrating the Metropolitan United Church at 56 Queen Street East this past Thursday evening.

I walked Toronto that Saturday with this information in my hand. By then I had begun my work at the museum, having completed a graduate degree in conservation. I was constantly handling old information. At work I was never concerned with the information itself but with the paper on which it was printed. Today it was the information that grabbed me, the blurry printout pinched in my hand, flapping in the breeze. Though my travels felt like aimless wandering, I descended straight down Yonge Street from the reference library, past the music shops, head shops, and strip clubs, all the way to Queen Street. I sat in the park at Queen and Church, staring up at the limestone tower of the Metropolitan, where a carillon of bells played. The soaring windows resonated music and sunlight, and I imagined a jagged puncture up there. It had been years since I'd discovered anything new in the family history.

It was a beautiful day in the sun and shadows of downtown, in a park full of vagrants surrounding the old church.

I contacted the archivist for the mental health hospital in Toronto, who directed me to the Archives of Ontario, where my search was a matter of filling in a form and writing a letter to plead my case: why did I want to know about this patient? They warned me that after a certain period, most files are destroyed, but some are archived. They warned me, also, that if George hadn't been dead for thirty years (or likely dead for thirty years), then they wouldn't be able to release whatever information they had. I included the clippings from the *Record* and *Telegram* with my letter.

I hit the jackpot. His casebook was in the archives. They released a copy of it to me.

I stared for many nights at those words, dates, names—the documents that defined my patrimony, and my father's. George sounded like my father, sounded like what I most feared becoming. He was certain of the ultimate truths of everything he saw. He was amazed that nobody else could understand the world as he did. He had a special gift that the world was not yet ready for.

George Anderson doesn't mention his son or his wife, though the doctor inquires of them at one point. George replies, "I have not a wife or a child, for all are my wives, my sons, my daughters, my brothers, sisters, fathers, and mothers."

I wanted Dad to know. I drove from Toronto on a Sunday afternoon and presented the evidence. He shook his head and placed both hands on his face, covering his mouth. I showed him records—legal, medical, death—of the life of George Anderson.

"Not true," he said. "Not true. You have been deceived."

I showed him again, explained it all again.

"Ha!" said Mom, who'd been listening in from the kitchen. "Who's a big shot now? Your father was a loon!"

Dad shook his head, his voice wavered with a feeble chuckle. "It's not true, none of it's true. The Deceiver has gotten to you."

"Dad, look, it's all—"

"You besmirch and lie and slander and you don't respect your family!" he said in his cornered animal squeal. "You are possessed."

I shut up, walked away, drove home saddened. My father had become a more real person the moment I saw the facts of my grandfather's life. And I saw my own delusion: I'd hoped some good would come of this. We never spoke of it again.

Dad's squeal was a warning to me: you don't want to deal with a father who has to deal with this.

FOURTEEN: *"Dad was christened at St. Andrew's Presbyterian Church..."*

Otterton, 1981 and earlier—My grandmother took Dad to the church she grew up in, but he stopped going when he began to study science, choosing rationally tested certainties over faith in the unprovable. In our house up until 1981, church and religion didn't exist. When our neighbours Mr. and Mrs. Fortino got into their car, dressed up on Sunday mornings, to go to the Catholic church, I had no clue where it was that they went.

It was not until Hillsview that I knew about religion, and that was where Dad would re-embrace it with a clinging hug. What better place than a church of infallible certainty?

But it was Mom who would find Jesus first.

On the night I was born again, when Mr. and Mrs. Crawford drove me home, I was in horrid fear of my parents toasting in the perpetual lake of fire. When they dropped me off, I prayed that Michael, my Mom's newfound boyfriend, wouldn't be there. All the lights were out.

"You okay going in there all by yourself?" said Mr. Crawford.

"Yes, uh, yes. Absolutely," I said. They looked at me over the back of their seat. "Praise the Lord," I added quickly.

"Praise the Lord," they said, and Mrs. Crawford reminded me to be back at church next week.

The house wasn't empty. The drawn curtains masked the faint glow of the muted television; its blue light revealed my mother as I opened the door. She lay on the floor, her face pale. She barely moved to acknowledge me.

"He's gone," she said.

"Michael?"

"Who else? Doesn't matter. He's gone."

I stood lifeless in the living room, staring at my mother.

The day after Dad left, Mom woke me with a wide-eyed smile, stirring a thick pink drink with frantic hands. In the kitchen, the table was covered in brochures and large containers of powder. "Did the phone ring last night?" I said. The bigger question hung unspoken, filling the space around us with doubt.

"Oh, that. Just a couple wrong numbers. Wrong numbers early in the morning." She gave me the drink. "We eat these for breakfast instead of cereal from now on," she said. "This drink is the future, and the future is healthy."

I took a sip and gagged. "It tastes like chalk!"

"No, dear, it tastes *de-li-cious*. And it helps people lose weight." She mixed another, clanging a dull chime in the glass.

"Where's Dad?" I finally asked.

She told me to put on my best clothes.

"Are we going somewhere?"

"From now on, everywhere *we* go is special, simply by the fact that we are there. We must always dress for success." She stared at me as though she could see straight through walls and all the way across the city. "Your father has gone away," she said in a calm voice, as though telling me we were out of toast. I saw the bags under her eyes, beyond the makeup. "One of the things I learned yesterday at the rally, the renewal rally," this formal name made what she said sound more true, "is that an obstacle is just an opportunity in disguise. So we have to grab this opportunity. It is a new day. A real man would join us in our crusade for health. Your father isn't a real man, but you can be, Billy, you make that choice and it will give you a future. When you have a future, there's no such thing as the past. That's another thing we talked about, and it's so true."

I'd woken up in another house—not completely different. It had the same rooms and pictures on the walls, but new rules now governed.

"He's gone," she said. "We move on. Put on your best clothes."

I changed from jeans to dark blue corduroys.

That was the day I stopped having friends. I was eleven years old and finished with the company of others. At the time it seemed the thing to do: hunker down.

Dad's departure from us was also my departure from the world of other people. Though I didn't know it yet, at least Dad would return soon enough.

While Mom embraced Dad's leaving, her two-and-a-half-week romance with Michael was a crushing defeat. Seeing her collapsed on the floor, I wanted my Jesus to help me help her but didn't know how to get Him into our living room. "Come over here," Mom said to me from where she lay on the floor. "Come be with your mother a while. It's so lonely."

As she clung to me and we watched *Falcon Crest*, I went for broke and whispered, "There is an answer."

She came to church the next week, and it was exactly like the week before except nothing was new to me and I felt no joy. Mom got the joy this time. When she jumped up and gave her heart to Jesus, I tried to be happy. I wanted to be happy; I stood at her side, crying by the altar because that was the most sincere thing to do, as she recited the same prayer from Pastor Haroldson. People would have thought that my tears were joyous, when really it was closer to heartbreak because whatever had washed over me the week before was not washing over me tonight. Where was the blood? I wanted precious shed blood and its power. Mom cried out in tongues, so loud and strong that everyone around her could hear.

The Crawfords drove us home after Mom chatted in the lobby while I stood by the door. She signed up five customers, two of whom asked her to mentor them so they could sell Slender Nation. It was the beginning of her walk with Jesus, and the moment that her business took off. Many people at Hillsview still eat the stuff today, and all the skinny ones sell it. This isn't as bad or as cynical as it sounds: people need community, however they can get it. Most people do, anyway. Not me, not then.

FIFTEEN: *"Surprises would upset Dad."*

Otterton, 1981, via Toronto, 2001—The phone rang at work a few weeks after the funeral, and I picked it up without thinking.

"William, Albert Haroldson here. How are you doing, son?"

I hung up. Ninety-seven fragments of the Book of the Dead lay on my table.

Jackie's fast-track approval of the restoration had proceeded as she'd hoped. She was like that. In a place full of genius, with many experts in things arcane, few were also as adept as her in handling the day-to-day business of getting things done. In a building full of thinkers, she was also slick. Where most of us would be handcuffed by needless worry, Jackie could glide through bureaucracy like a figure skater.

I was working under a tent in the middle of my lab— to further control humidity—laying out the most bent and deformed pieces of scroll, letting these drink in the air until malleable. I was bending them back to flat.

There was urgency to this work. I was to receive a visitor very soon. Jackie had contacted a German university where scholars had dedicated their lives to studying the Book of the Dead.

The visitor's name was Berthe, and this was her final project before retiring. For more than forty years she'd been studying scrolls and fragments of scrolls. In anticipation of her arrival, my lab was visited no less than seven times in two days, mostly by Bob and Jackie, but also the museum president with two trustees, a fundraiser, and another conservator. I was ready to bolt the door. The attention and the urgency were destroying my peace with the paper, my solitude.

When Berthe arrived I was stunned. For a sixty-seven-year-old woman, Berthe looked thirty, with a child's playfulness in her face. Perhaps this was also because she was barely five feet tall. Standing next to me, the top of her head was three inches above my elbow. Standing next to Bob, she looked like a kid.

For ten days, Berthe and I worked together numbering and photographing every last fragment.

"What're we doing next?" I said as she prepared to leave, my stomach raging, my hand touching the foil roll of antacids in my pocket.

"That's with me now, yeah."

"What are you going to do?"

"I have now a big, uh, puzzle. I'll print these and cut them out, so I have all the same pieces as you do here, and I'll put them together."

"And then we'll have a complete scroll."

"Nah. There will be gaps. Sure. Always gaps."

Berthe returned to Germany to assemble her puzzle. While she was gone, it was up to me to come up with a design for mounting the scroll in a way that would preserve it and also allow for display from time to time. An exhibit had been hastily scheduled. We had very little time to get it done.

The flashing light on my office phone blinked its red warning. If it was a museum person, I'd return the call the next day. I stared at the red light, wanting to upend the table, throw the fire alarm to trigger the sprinklers, drop the fragments into the shredder. Without meaning to, I began to time travel.

It was 1981. Dad had been gone several weeks, and Slender Nation was going nowhere except into our stomachs, despite Mom's speeches and meetings. I was hiding out in my basement fort, looking at my favourite plane. It was a bomber, a Flying Fortress that actually flew through the air on wings of Styrofoam, powered by rubber band engines. I carefully took it down from the shelf. I pulled out three books of matches, cut off the heads, and stuffed the match heads into the plane. I would make it explode, just like in a war movie.

Upstairs, Mom was practising. I put the plane down and listened to the slogan: "Good luck is just a good plan, hard work, and the patience to see it through." She clapped, simulating great applause. I loaded up my bomber.

The next night, with the house at my back, facing the power line field and the dying sun, I stood on the brown and flattened grass, wound the engines, and lit my homemade fuse. The plane took off as I tossed it forward. It hummed beautifully and flew arrow straight for a moment before turning in a slow arc. I watched in growing fear as it looped around toward the house and slammed into the dining room patio doors in an explosion of orange flares.

Moments later Mom ran out, screaming, followed by two people she'd invited over to try Slender Nation. She emptied the kitchen fire extinguisher onto the last of my model plane. She stepped back from the mess and, holding the empty extinguisher in one hand, fixed her hair and adjusted her pink button with the other. She looked over to me, twenty feet away, cleared her throat and said, "Billy, you have interrupted us and taken away time that I wanted to spend with my friends. We have important business to discuss tonight."

Her prospects—a tall woman and a grey-haired man standing behind her—looked away. The man shuffled his feet. "We're going back inside," she said, adjusting her skirt as she placed the extinguisher down. "Stay out here and clean this up." They went in. As I climbed onto the deck, she pulled the patio curtains shut from the inside.

Two days later she announced at breakfast, "Billy, I have a surprise and you are going to love it." She tapped her fingers together.

"What is it?"

"Well, I've been thinking. You *are* a boy and you're a very good boy, but it would be really good for you to meet other boys."

"There are boys at school."

"Yes, but I think it would also be nice for you to be around men."

"There are men teachers at school. And there's men who come to your meetings."

"Yes, dear. That's true too, but what I'm talking about is maybe someone who could look out for you, you know, be a father figure," she said with the same twitchy smile she made when asking me about my classes. The words *father figure* made me feel sick inside.

"I have a dad."

"Yes, but you have to move on, and maybe it's okay to have other friends who are like dads. I applied for you to be in a special group called Dad to Lend. You have been matched up with a Dad to Lend named Michael Bentley, and he's coming here tonight to take you to a special gathering. There'll be lots of people and you can all be friends."

Behind the school, there was an island in the middle of the concrete yard. The island was made up of five trees, surrounded by earth, forming a small circle of dirt in the pavement. The island made me invisible and safe. I made the concrete into the ocean, and the island my refuge when I wanted to be alone. The other kids played in the ocean while I walked in my five-tree forest or sat on my beach. I liked the smell of the earth and the feeling of the slick bark when I touched it. I would trace my hand over and over again across the knotholes where branches had been cut away, across the blemishes in the tree skin, across the carved hearts and initials engraved over many years. I didn't even know who these people were, but the trees said they were in love.

Sitting on the island that morning, I talked myself into thinking Dad to Lend was a good idea. I promised myself that it was only for a little while. When Dad came home, I wouldn't have to go anymore, and I would be able to tell him that that was my plan from the start.

Dad to Lend turned out to be as stupid as it sounds. I went one time and hated it. Michael was okay, a nice guy I guess, but I didn't want to hang out with him. I needed a way out, but Mom told me I was not allowed to quit.

Next week came and I stole money from Mom's purse while she led a renewal rally. I called Michael and quietly told him that I was never coming to Dad to Lend again, thank you. I went out into the night, leaving Mom a note that I was off to Dad to Lend and was meeting up with Michael there.

As I stepped out the door, I heard from the living room the surprised voices of Mom's visitors as they learned that their promised free dinner was merely a shake. I was drinking Slender Nation religiously and still wanted to believe everyone else should too.

I walked up Belting Court to the bus stop, floating along in time with the lightly falling snow. Snow made the air different. Tonight it felt clean, but if it had been warmer it would have smelled of muddy rot. The stolen money in my pocket made me rich, along with two one-dollar bills I'd been saving for my next model.

The lights from a bus pulled into view from around a distant corner. I sat at the front, across from an old lady with a shopping cart. The driver kept looking at me, like I shouldn't be out by myself. I recognized him from trips I'd taken with Mom. She'd pitched Slender Nation to him, but he cut her off mid-sentence, "Sorry, lady. No moon-lighting. Union rules." This reminded me of spray-painted scrawl behind the school, "Zeppelin Rules."

Soon the lights of the mall glowed before me, the out-of-synch bus windshield wipers clearing the view. The mall sat parallel to the road at the back of a parking lot ten cars deep. It was a strip of nine storefronts with a sheltered sidewalk, plus a grocery store at the end. I exited the bus and crossed the lot. The wide arc of light from each street lamp lit up the snow in conical beams. My gaze became fixed on the flashing sign of Captain Arcade: black letters on a white background that blinked until it was impossible to ignore.

Though drawn, desperately, toward the arcade, I couldn't walk directly to it. Instead I went toward Mike's

Place, the convenience store two doors down. To the right of Mike's was Presto Pizza, where Dad had sometimes taken me, long ago, before he left, before everything, before Slender Nation. Farther on were a doctor's office and a dentist and a place called The Midnight Club, then a small break in the sidewalk before the grocery store.

Mom had warned me many times to never go into Captain Arcade, that merely being there would make me want to take drugs, and that I'd also get stabbed. I walked the bright aisles of Mike's Place considering this possibility, passing rows of food that would be tasty but so very, very bad. I quietly condemned all the food. I wouldn't touch it, wouldn't break my vow to Slender Nation though I hated the stuff. I passed by bubble gum, chips, and candy bars, seeing these with the corner of my eye as I stared at the floor. I hurried from the store. Captain Arcade beckoned. I turned away and walked to the end of the mall and stood in front of The Midnight Club.

The windows were black. Music thumped within. A stark sign read, "Age of Majority Strictly Enforced. You must be nineteen years or older to enter." A jacked-up, chrome-laden Duster pulled up, fishtailing in the snow, and three men jumped out. They were rough looking, two with moustaches, all with hair flowing long down their necks. They walked past me into the club. The thumping became a screaming wail as they opened the door. I tried to see inside, while pretending not to look, but saw nothing. The sounds faded. I walked hurriedly to the arcade.

At the doorway I stopped to feel if my brain was being reprogrammed, to sense getting stoned by touching the door handle, thinking these may be the last real thoughts I might ever have and that maybe it would be better that way.

A man appeared along the sidewalk. He stepped up to me in a wooly coat and said, "Do you know the answer?" as he handed over the small blue piece of paper that would lead me, a few days later, to Hillsview Independent Pentecostal. I stuffed the paper in my back pocket and turned away from him. The arcade had a warning sign, similar in size to the one at The Midnight Club, but all it said was "No minors allowed during school hours." Relieved that I was breaking no rule, I pulled the door open and was buried in a pile of noise.

Everyone was big, bigger than I'd ever be, with the mysterious toughened teenage look that was so fascinating to me. The walls, floors, and ceilings were all the same dark blue, almost black. The place smelled part movie theatre and part hockey rink—smoke mixed with packed-in bodies. To the right and left through the darkness were lines of glowing video games in big cabinets against the walls, the only light except for the pinball machines and a jukebox at the back, bright but silent. Up and down the rows of machines, high school kids leaned into the screens without blinking. They reeled, sucked air, threw their bodies from side to side, swayed in close then away, with every jerking movement of the controls, with every press of a button.

I went to a game that simulated racing a car at night. It had a driver's seat, steering wheel, gearshift, and pedals. I sat down and leaned back against the hard plastic. My feet barely reached the pedals. I stepped out casually, as though passing through on a shortcut to another destination. A man with a missing front tooth and an apron full of quarters gave out change. Crazy sounds all around—beeps, explosions, sirens, and bells. I'd fallen from the sky into a jungle where I watched out for snakes and wild animals, a landed alien in a room full of space invaders.

A teenaged boy smacked the side of a machine.

"Cut it or you're gone!" yelled the man with the missing tooth. Every few moments somebody yelled "Fuck!" or "Yes!"

Pinball machines, so ancient and funny looking compared to video games, lined the back of the room with their lights and big silver balls and ringing bells. I stared at the flashing police light on top of a pinball machine as it suddenly let out a siren wail. Next to it, another machine was covered with pictures of women in bikinis, who lit up brightly in a random order, their eyes and teeth especially bright, their breasts large enough to make them fall over. I'd watched Dad try to play pinball once, at Presto Pizza. We'd been waiting to pick up dinner, and I begged him to play it until he finally dropped a quarter in. As he began to slowly run his finger along the instructions, I hit the red button to start the game. His face flushed as red as that button. "You can't start until you know what you're doing. That's why we need to read the instructions," he barked. I smacked the machine. It tilted. The game was over, and so began one of his lectures on comportment.

I went to the man with the missing tooth and held out my money. He rolled eight quarters into my hand. Walking the rows of games, I looked closely at the ones nobody was playing and passed by a crowd—at least ten people—surrounding *Defender*. They kept reacting together, saying, "Ooh!" or "Nice!" or "Yesss!"

At empty machines, game demos played on loop, enticing quarters from my pocket. I went to each empty machine, one by one, and put my hands on the controls to pretend I was playing. Pretending was harder than playing; when you played the game, you were in control. Pretending, I had to time my moves perfectly to make it look like I was in command.

A few minutes at each machine was all I needed to memorize the demo and fake my way. I deepened the authenticity by growing angry at the exact moment of death, saying "Drat!" each time it happened, too shy to say "Fuck!" I demoed through lives and deaths at *Galaga*, *Pac-Man*, *Donkey Kong*, and *Galaxian*. It cost nothing.

I'd almost mastered the demo for *Dig Dug*, tunnelling along underground and warding off bad guys, when I sensed someone next to me. I turned to see Ian Stonehouse, a grade-eight street thug from my school. Ian was one of the cool kids, tanned and blond, already more man than boy, who never seemed to do anything except hang around across the street from the school, smoking cigarettes and looking mean. "Stone" was a stranger to me, a tough. He looked at me like I was a moron. "You're a friggin' knob," he said, "the games work if you put a quarter in."

"I know."

"Then play it!" He slammed his hand down on the top of the cabinet. I reached for a quarter with my shaking hand, fearing he might steal it, and dropped it in. I pressed the start button and the opening music played. Beneath my winter coat my shirt soaked through with sweat. I lasted five seconds in my first life. My second was even shorter. Stone laughed at me.

"Man, I'm never this bad," I mumbled in pale fakery.

"Why you making so many stupid moves?" he said. He leaned in close enough that I could smell the half-eaten bag of chips in his jean jacket pocket, and the smell made me instantly full of the craving that The Slender Nation sales manual called false hunger.

On my third turn I did only slightly better. Stone smacked me on the side of my head, crumpling my ear in sharp radiant pain. "Melvin fucking nerd." I fought off the watering in my eyes and stared at the screen, trying to come up with things to say back to him. I thought of none.

"Hey, that'll cost you a quarter!" he said.

"What?"

"My advice. I don't give it out for free. Pay up."

I noticed a group of kids gawking from a distance. He frowned. "Pay up."

"But, for wha—"

Stone burst out laughing, as did his friends. He walked away slowly, leaving me alone with my hands on the machine. "D'you fuckin' see 'em? He was gonna do it. I betcha he was gonna pay." One of his friends, a skinny guy with a striped shirt, yelled over, "Hey, yeah and you owe me two bucks rent for standing there." I laughed, quietly helpless; it was what I thought I was supposed to do, pretend I was in on it all along.

I skulked away to another game at the far end of the arcade, hearing that voice trail after me, "You owe me my rent. You owe me my rent."

This game had aliens attacking me as I flew a supersonic fighter plane. I promptly exploded three times in a row. "Game Over" flashed on the screen. I fantasized about punching the guy who said I owed rent. I spent another quarter. Same result. I counted the money in my pocket with my fingers. I'd lost so much in only a few minutes. For a few dollars I could buy a model plane that would keep me busy for weeks. But models were for little kids. I should stop wanting them.

But I was not ready to leave, not while they thought I was scared. I walked to the semi-circle around *Defender*, which now included Stone and his friends, and edged my way through the group to get a closer look. A tall, denim-clad high school kid with dirty blond hair stared at the screen, entranced. He shot aliens and saved falling humans, his hands dancing across the many buttons of the console in an elegant, dizzying, complicated rhythm, as though playing piano. And next to him was the legendary Ross Marlborough, track star and jumper of Blue Rock Falls. I leaned in for a closer look, when a hand on the back of my jacket collar yanked me backwards. It was Stone. "Darryl's been on the same game since noon. He's goin' for a new record. Don't fuckin' crowd him."

Stone said this more like advice than a threat, and I knew he wouldn't demand my money, not next to Darryl, the man who humbled and diminished all, even Ian Stonehouse.

"Seven hours on one quarter," I said in awe.

"Yeah. Exactly," said Stone. "Ross's stepping in when Darryl goes to the can, and I'm gonna help too if he needs it." Darryl looked so focused yet so calm it'd be hard to believe he was playing at all if you didn't look at his hands. And yet despite his calm, a frill of energy shimmered around him, as though his body was vibrating, a guitar string tuned too high, threatening to pling with an off-key note. "Hey Darryl, you need another pack of smokes?" said Stone. Darryl shook his head, just barely. A burning cigarette with an inch-long line of ash rested on the machine next to his left thumb, which tapped and hovered over the reverse button.

"He's already rolled the machine over twice. That's a million points each time. It's fuckin' awesome." Stone was flushed, the proud inside guy with Darryl, and I was thrilled that he'd even speak to me. The screen showed forty-six extra lives. I shook my head, checking for brain damage, wondering if now I would want to take drugs.

Darryl's tally climbed higher and higher, inching its way toward another million point rollover. At 990,000, he started gaining an extra life with every single hit. He worked furiously, muttering, "Got to get one hundred before the roll. Have to do it before the roll." He flicked the ash-heavy cigarette to the carpet, where its last embers slowly faded to nothing. I wanted to stomp on it but feared stepping too close to the game. People hooted and cheered as the count of extra lives went higher and higher, "Fuckin' right, Darryl. Fuckin' right."

"Go Darryl. Go man. Go for it."

The score reset to zero, with the screen showing nine-ty-eight extra lives. I slipped away as the cheers peaked and Darryl played on. The Dad to Lend gathering I was supposedly at would be ending soon, so would the renewal rally. All my money would be gone if I played any more games. How could I become as good as Darryl? To play all day on one quarter, to have a crowd watch and cheer for me? I'd need to spend a fortune in order to one day play for free. I had to leave. And I had to pee.

Feeling my way down a dim corridor at the back of the arcade, I inched toward the red glow of a fire exit. My hand found a side door just before the exit. This had to be the bathroom. I tried the handle, but it was locked. Feeling along the wall in the dark, I found a light switch covered in tape. I pulled off the tape and flicked the switch.

The arcade snapped silent. From up the hallway came nothing but empty darkness, not a sound or light from any of the games. A chorus of groans rose up, over which Darryl shrieked, "Fuck! Holy fuck what happened I was heading for a world fucking record high fucking score. Fuck!"

I ran out the fire door and down the alley, my shoes slipping in slush that soaked through to my socks, to a side street and up to the main road where I kept running until I'd passed three bus stops. When I couldn't go far-ther I stopped, panting, with my hands on my knees. In my pocket I found the reassurance of my last quarters and bus ticket. Stepping away from the light of a streetlamp, I peed in the darkness against a fence. As the steam rose, I tried not to admit to myself how great it felt to shut the place down. There was power in that switch.

Waiting for the bus, I imagined Darryl leading a posse into the night to hunt down the switch thrower.

At home the house was quiet, dark, and locked. I let myself in with my key. Mom had left a note on the table:

Billy,

I'm writing this in the hope that you come home and have not been murdered or run over by a truck. I've gone with Michael to look for you. He and I need to talk with you about this stunt you have done. He called after you left. I had to cut the renewal rally short because of you. Tonight was the night when everything was going to take off. This will cost us and that was an awful thing you did to him. You're acting like your father. You better be ready to explain where you were tonight.

I dropped the note back on the table. Somewhere Mom and Michael the Dad to Lend were making plans and schemes for me. I'd have rather been beaten up by Darryl.

The darkened house grew quieter. It was eight thirty and nobody was there to watch over me, but this did not matter; I could do whatever I wanted in my basement fort every day. The faucet in the bathroom dripped a steady plink, plink, plink. I tried to stop it by wrenching the knob over. It plinked on, slightly slower. I thought of watching TV, but that would put me front and centre the moment she returned.

I quickly changed into pajamas, brushed my teeth, climbed into bed, shut the light, and in the darkness tried to wish everything away. This was safer than waiting up for her.

I needed a story: I went out to buy a model plane, no, something for her—a Christmas present. The thought of doing this filled me for a moment with warmth, the joy of considering something charitable. I checked the clock: 9:17 p.m. Maybe she'd left for good. Maybe I'd given her reason to leave for a long time. This seemed less scary than facing her when she came home.

I lay awake for hours, and still she didn't return. I listened to the sounds of the house, imagining how I'd live if she did not come back. When was it official? At what point was I officially an orphan? Would it be midnight or did my status change come morning? I got up. A creak in the hallway floor made me whirl around. Nothing there, but it was amazing how much I could see in the dark. The Slender Nation clock beamed 11:37 p.m. I'd never been up at midnight before—it nearly happened one year on December 31, but my parents got into a fight over whether it was good for me to see New Year's and I went to bed at 10:42 p.m. Still, Mom and Michael were somewhere, planning my execution, or maybe he'd kidnapped her! I grabbed her note, still on the kitchen table, and read it again. The words *like your father* burned up at me even though I could barely read in the shadowy light. Dad had nothing to do with what I'd done, and Mom had already disappeared with the new unknown man, probably forever. I picked up the note and stuffed it into my pajama pants. Nothing was wrong with Dad, except that he was probably gone because of me. So much was wrong with me, though. I was bad at video games, I hated Slender Nation, and the mystery of what pushed Dad away consumed me.

The front door opened, and I couldn't breathe. I imagined a burglar coming to take Mom's Slender Nation supplies and all of my models. I imagined Michael locking up Mom and coming back for me using her keys.

It was Mom, hair full of snow. Her face glowed in the hallway light as she flicked the switch, blinding me for a moment. In my relief at her return, I expected her to slap me. Instead, she spun around slowly as she took off her coat and lobbed it toward the closet, her arm outstretched as the coat landed with a thump, as though the point of her finger had guided it to its resting place. With this pose and a massive smile, she looked like she was dreaming of being a dancer. "Oh, poor dear," she said as she noticed me, "you're scared." Dropping to her knees, she clasped her hands, still cold from outside, on my cheeks. "I didn't mean to go for so long, but we got to talking. And I didn't know where you went. I was so worried, and mad, but Michael explained that you were probably just fine—testing your wings, right? Well, I guess that's how you learn." I nodded, stunned, unsure if she was going to hug me. She did not.

"And Billy, I have some exciting news," she said as she stood and twirled past me to the kitchen. "Michael's going to work with me in Slender Nation, so we'll both get to see him a lot more. Isn't that wonderful?"

Yes, before leading our family to our saviour, I brought Mom to her one brief romance.

In front of me, fragments of the Book crawled under my skin from where they lay on the museum table, and I trembled with the tingling memory of shutting down Darryl the Magnificent. Out in the hallway, movement and conversation, people happy to be going home, people talking about politics or the latest news, people talking about their kids. Five o'clock, I should leave too. I didn't trust myself alone here right now. The scroll was inching its way toward the shredder. I couldn't care one way or another about the things people talked about; I just wanted my solitude. Berthe had been okay to work with, and now we communicated mostly by email. My détente with Bob and Jackie was manageable: they'd drop in, I'd show them what's what, and they'd leave. It was everybody else that came clawing that started to get to me. I knew I didn't own the lab, but for years I'd lived in quiet anonymity as I fixed book bindings, checked the fastness of ink, unrolled scrolls, and rolled scrolls back up. It was calm delight. Each page changed as my eye penetrated its makeup, transforming it from smooth surface to a vast rolling cellulose prairie with occasional ditches and hills, or a cratered moon, and I interpreted what that prairie, that moon, said about the stability of the paper. With the Book of the Dead in front of me, my solitude was gone. I couldn't go an hour without being visited by an eager higher-up or a curious co-worker or a trustee or a donor. They oohed and fawned over the little scraps of the Book of the Dead, always asking me the same questions. How old is it? What's it worth? Can it be *saved*? I gave the same answers politely and waited for them to leave. People never asked about the fibres, the mesh, the chemical composition, the intricacies of restoration. Instead they marvelled at the *oldness* of the Book. But did any of them stop to think about the true amazement: documents are temporary. What's a twenty-four-hundred-year-old scrappy scroll mean in the billions of years of the universe? I wanted back to my long, slow, lonely love with the touch and feel and construction of paper.

I packed up. I wanted the gallery watchers to go away. I was a zoo animal.

At home, I pulled from my briefcase a medium-sized scrap from the Book of the Dead, about the size of a Post-it note. It was my contraband for the evening and this excited me. I'd never absconded with an artifact before. Giddily, I held it with bare fingers, by the edges at first, then let my thumb brush briefly across its surface. I turned it over and over and over in my hands, my body tensing in a hush of anticipation. I turned the water on in

135

the sink and passed the scrap from hand to hand, stomping my feet, until I could stand it no more.

After, I whipped my legs with a belt until I bled. The next day, I returned the fragment to the museum and also brought with me a whip to keep hidden in the lab. If I needed relief, I'd need it fast.

SIXTEEN: *"... he began work in the Meteorological Office of Environment Canada"*

Otterton, 1977–1982—When I was seven, Dad gave Mom a sweater for her birthday, red and blue with jagged designs, and he helped me make her a card. The sweater made her frown. "It's not for me," she said. "It's not right for me." He insisted she try it on.

"Have another look in the mirror," said Dad.

She frowned. "No, it's not for me. Take it back."

"They won't take it back, Janet," he said. "I'm certain they won't take it back."

We drove to the mall, the two of them silent, Mom scowling and Dad looking hurt. "Leave it with me," she'd said, swinging open the car door as she left us in the parking lot.

She was gone a while, and it got too hot to sit inside listening to the radio. We got out. I stared at the ground. Dad stared at the sky.

"It's going to rain," he said. "Cold. Cold rain the next two, three days." He squinted up at the high wispy clouds.

"It's sunny," I said, kicking a piece of gravel across the concrete. It rolled up by his feet. He kicked it back to me.

We played rock soccer until the stone came to rest against the thick tires of a dusty yellow sedan. Dad redirected his gaze upwards.

"Those are wind-torn clouds, ripped high cirrus clouds. See them, all up there," he said, pointing with his small finger, the rest of his hand closed in a fist. "You only get clouds like that on good weather days, just before it goes bad. They're being pushed by strong winds, high in the jet stream. Those winds will come down to where we are. The weather's going to change." Dad was the smartest person in the world, the most grown-up of all adults. He had big words and knew what they meant and I clung to those words.

Mom reappeared. "They tried to give me that same no refund garbage, but I found a manager, and what do you know, we've got our twenty dollars back!" she said with a proud smile. "I can always get a money-back guarantee." Dad looked away. She never thanked him for the gift.

By evening the next day a big storm came in. It rained for two days.

Randomness was unacceptable to Dad. Predicting weather gave him command which he found nowhere else. He craved certainty, which to him meant truth. If he knew when rain should begin, he could get through the day. Days when the forecast showed variability were especially troubling to him.

When I was eight my teacher, Mrs. Dvorshak, assigned

our class the project "My Mom and Dad at Work."

Mom was easy: two days a week she went to the high school, where she was a secretary. It couldn't be any simpler. We saw the secretaries in the office at our own school, and Mom didn't conjure any mystique about it. "It's a job, makes some bucks and gets me out of the house," she said. "I can't sit around here all day; I'd go crazy."

Dad, however, wore a grey suit and carried a briefcase. He left each morning at 8:25 a.m. and returned at 5:15 p.m. unless he had to work late because of meetings. The phonetics of *meeting* made me imagine a group of men around a table eating steak.

This was his pattern except on those days when he didn't get up because he was tired, days that sometimes stretched into weeks, or into sickness. I never heard him cough or sneeze or throw up when he was sick. He would snore.

For the project, I asked him what he did. I copied down his words, asking him to spell out the ones I didn't know. I nodded gravely and took the information to my room and my dictionary, awed by his brilliance.

I repeated his words verbatim in front of the class, knees trembling in my finest corduroy, brimming with pride: "My Dad develops and evaluates statistical models for prescribed data applications for the Environment Canada predictions centre. Most of these are more than 97 percent accurate, which is far superior to any other model. They are so accurate that they are now applied across the country, and some are used internationally as well." Dying to see the rapt curiosity of my classmates, I looked momentarily up from my pages to stony faces of bored confusion and the smirk of a girl stifling a giggle. I plodded on.

When I was finished a kid named Andre, who was an asshole, asked, "What's that mean?" I filled with fury.

Dad could have said, "I'm a weatherman—not the one on TV, but one who helps the man on TV know what to say." But to be understood was not for him. He had to be the only one who could understand what he knew. It was another of his ways of getting by.

I showed my presentation to Mom, telling her how it had been questioned. "He's a pompous idiot," she said.

"Andre?"

"No, your father." She said the same to him directly when he arrived in his grey suit, following him around the house with badgering remarks. He didn't put down his briefcase or take off his shoes. He said nothing back to her. He let go with one of his shrieks. Later, he sought me out in my room.

"Your mother is ignorant and hysterical. Her comprehension of the world is minimal, and her ability to discern and synthesize information is inexistent. Be careful, you don't want to be like that."

This too, I wrote down, in phonetic scribbles, so I could look up the correct spellings and definitions later.

During the frail and tenuous months after Dad came back and first joined the church—the months when I still desperately sought to feel the joy of being saved again, the months before I broke away—Dad and I spent a weekend at a father-son retreat with Pastor Haroldson, Mr. Crawford, and a bunch of other Hillsviewites, young and old.

We were to travel by bus to the camp on a Saturday, after meeting up in the church parking lot. I was worried on the drive to the church, worried about where I stood with God, but the worry mixed with the excitement offered by a weekend in the woods.

I remember Dad wanting to fit in with the other men. I see him shifting on his feet, standing to the outside of a shoulder-to-shoulder circle of fathers in the church parking lot, making a small bump in their roundness with me right behind him. We stood next to the school bus painted white and burgundy (white for purity of Jesus, burgundy for us being representatives of royalty—the King of Kings).

I lingered with him as the men spoke about how long the drive to camp would be. "It'll be clear all weekend," Dad said, peering upward as eyes turned to him. "You can tell by the height of the cumulonimbus clouds." Dad's hopeful smile, the way he looked at the group, was like a kid waiting to be picked for a team. They went silent, and the circle soon broke up without any more conversation.

Later, as we drove, singing "He Touched Me" and "Each of Us a Cross to Bear," Dad grew worried, looking out through the grey filter of the tinted windows. "It's overcast," he said with an anxious nod. "The weather is wrong. It's supposed to be clear. Something's gone wrong. I told them it would be fine."

We turned onto a side road marked "Love of Jesus Camp. Private Property of Hillsview Independent Pentecostal Fellowship and Ministry. NO TRESPASSING."

Camp was less an adventure and more an all-day, all-night church service populated by men and boys. Sleeping cabins radiated around the edge of a clearing, at the centre of which was a steel barn-like structure, a central hall where we ate our meals and attended endless hymn sing and worship services.

The other sons fell into two groups: much younger— primary school children of seven and eight years old, who were given their own Sunday school type program, and much older—teenagers who were expected to spend all their time with the men. The only other kid even close to my age was, terrifyingly, Ian Stonehouse.

At the first break in the day, Ian walked straight to me. "You're Billy, you go to Crestwood." I stammered a yes, unnerved that he'd remembered me. "You came to the arcade one night."

"Yeah." I was certain he was going to bust me for throwing the switch.

"This place blows," he said, and I nodded, clueless as to what he meant, not daring to disagree. "Hey, I could tell the whole school you were at this stupid thing."

"And how would you tell them without telling them you were here too?" I said, trying to follow his logic, realizing as I said it that I was threatening him.

"Yeah. I get it," he said. "This place still blows though."

"I didn't know you were saved," I said, sounding ridiculous. If I hadn't really believed in salvation the first time, it would have been easy to talk casually about this. But I had believed, and I still wanted to believe. My voice sounded feeble and fake.

He grimaced. "Saved, eh? Well, aren't we all?" He rolled his eyes. "Hey, stick with me later on—there's a break after dinner."

Turned out that Ian's father, since getting out of jail, had found Jesus. They were spending their monthly weekend together at the retreat.

The day went on with more singing, sermons, and testimony. Fathers and a few teenaged sons, all standing and talking about how they were brought back from the depths, saved from demons, healed of unworthiness, allowed to see sunshine for the first time in their lives by being saved. One of the fathers, a man of few words named Jim, got up and spoke of "having personal relations with Jesus." Next to me I could feel the stories having a magnetic pull on Dad. What I didn't know was whether he was trying to get up the nerve to testify. And I didn't know what sins he'd been saved from.

At the evening break, Ian found me and brought me along with a nudge. We walked off in the dark beyond the clearing and sat on a log on a slow rise that looked down into the camp. "So much bullshit," he said. "Everybody here's a loser, except my dad." He pulled out a thin, squat bottle and twisted off the cap. "Vodka," he said. "Snuck it from my mom. Perfect for here—nobody can smell it on you." I took a couple sips, cool and searing on the mouth and throat, and waited for the mystical feeling of being drunk, which never came. He took many gulps in the darkness and finished off the bottle, tucking the empty into his jean jacket.

What came to me instead of the hoped-for drunken buzz was a new layer of sin paranoia. Alcohol was yet another of the evils railed against at church, along with tobacco, slothfulness, mendacity, lasciviousness, covetousness, video games, and a host of other evils. I'd never make it to heaven.

Ian was less troubled by eternity. He handed me two sticks of gum as we walked to the hall, him with more swagger than usual. "Chew 'em well," he said.

"I thought you can't smell this stuff."

"Just chew 'em and don't goof up in there. I don't need any grief from my old man. Got it?"

"Got it."

We strode into the stark brightness of the hall, and Ian threw his arms in the air, the way of praising God that was normal at Hillsview. He hung up his coat and began to shout, barrelling up the aisle to the delight of his father and Pastor Haroldson and the other men, bellowing "Praise the Lord. Praise him, praise him, praise him. Praise. Him!"

The crowd began clapping and singing, and he was on the stage, alive in the spirit as they say, waving and jumping and exhorting as arms waved back at him across the hall. Ian Stonehouse, thirteen years old, drunken tough guy and spiritual wunderkind. I sat quietly next to my father, who watched Ian's fervour.

I looked away. To my horror, Ian's jacket hung wide open on the wall, the vodka bottle in full view and threatening to fall to the floor and smash. He would be caught; *we* might be caught. As he spoke from the stage in wailing tongues, I slipped to the back of the room and carefully took the jacket down, folding it over to cover the bottle.

He charged up and down the stage, arms waving wildly, his face alight. The pastor was next to him with his arms in the air, and Ian was screaming, "Who's on fire? Who's on fire for Jesus? Who knows it in their heart? Who knows it?"

Not me was the honest voice I heard within, but it wasn't for lack of wanting it. I wanted to be on fire. I wanted to be Ian, and I wanted to be true to God, and I wanted to know if there was any difference. And I wanted that feeling again, and the more he yelled, high-fiving the men like a sports hero, the meaner I became.

I slipped away to the back of the room again, where I hung his coat back up, turning it around as before so that the bottle was in plain view, a beacon.

The service went on, one song droning into another sermon into another testimony. I thought about that bottle. Was it right or wrong to do what I'd done? I could argue both sides evenly. Should I hide it again? No, too risky. I was just being honest.

When the night was finally over, after the long last prayer, we began to file out and the commotion finally came. "What the HELL is this?" yelled Mr. Stonehouse, holding the bottle out to Ian, who shrugged. Mr. Stonehouse closed his eyes, "Forgive me Lord, for swearing, Hell is a real place, I know. Protect me from it." He opened his eyes, grabbed his son by the arm and, twisting it around his back, he hauled Ian away. Ian didn't make a sound.

That night, I lay in my bunk surfing the high of power —I made something happen—and the heaviness of guilt—I betrayed Ian. I told myself I'd done nothing wrong, that putting the bottle on display was merely repairing my dishonesty for hiding it in the first place. But the wincing sneer on Ian's face, biting his lip as his father twisted his arm, that sneer would not leave me. I tried to tell myself I was serving God by making sure he got caught.

My father said, "You know that boy, Ian, right? Is he your friend?"

"Kinda, I know him I guess."

"I'm glad you didn't do what he did tonight—drinking alcohol and all that."

"Thanks," I said.

"But if you did, son, I could understand, because really it would be your mother's fault if you acted that way."

As we boarded the bus the next day, Ian was waiting for me. All he said was, "Look just cause we hung out here doesn't mean we're friends back at school. Got it?"

I got it.

SEVENTEEN: *"...his office was closed by cutbacks in 1995."*

Otterton, 1995—Dad didn't rail against the closing or the loss of his job but, rather, against the terminology of his termination: he was declared redundant.

This was impossible. He was unique, from an important family, a founding pillar of the community. Nobody was like him or his ancestry. Nobody!

He raged for days, then weeks, spurred by my mother whose rejoinder to his every complaint was "Go get another job."

Dad added the government to the list of those who'd stolen his life, and began volunteering full time at Hillsview. The church became his home, and the anonymous faceless government became the object of his rage, the stand-in, until the end, for everything and everyone that taunted and tormented him, a bureaucratic embodiment of the demonic.

EIGHTEEN: *"He was a hard person to get to know."*

Otterton, 1998 and earlier—His kindness was a slow suf-focating crush.

A close look at Dad's smile showed clenched teeth. His affinity for grief could steer any conversation to forebears who were cheated despite their greatness or because of their greatness, to how they died, and then to a recount-ing of what he was doing when he'd heard. He could do this for ancestors back to the 1840s, providing lengthy explanations of the significance of the deceased. "Your great-great-uncle Stockton would have become the fin-est railroad engineer of his day were it not for the acci-dent that blinded him in his right eye. It was the fault of a negligent signalman. His left eye was too weak. He couldn't go on. He died soon after. It was 1887, and the railroad ruled the land..." Dad's voice would trail away in grieving tremor. "Your grandmother told me that story when I was seven years old, and I'll never forget it. I was playing with a toy bear." Forebears were all glorious, and wronged. This was his way, and he wouldn't allow any-thing to upset his patterns.

For his birthday one year, not long after I took my job

at the museum, I bought him a weekend at a lodge. Only much later would I realize how this mimicked (and perhaps tried to make right) the slow agony of our weekend at Love of Jesus Camp.

He stared at the gift certificate, holding it delicately with two hands as though the faux parchment was the real thing and I should have presented it wearing the white cotton gloves I use at work. Mom crowded in, looking over his shoulder, reading aloud the details, "One weekend at Trout Lake Lodge. Fishing and hunting (in season), hiking, snowshoeing, snowmobiling, all meals included."

"Out of my light!" said Dad, swatting backward with his hand, as he did when anyone stood close to him. He looked the paper up and down, frowning. "Do we have to do all of these things if we stay there?" he said with grave concern. And did they have a church at the lodge? And was it a true church, a new church washed in the spirit and not one of those impostors like the Catholics, Anglicans, Presbyterians, or Uniteds? And were we obligated to eat their food or could he bring his own? He would get very, very sick, quickly, if he didn't keep up his regimen of Slender Nation.

And, his anxiety rising as mine rose in reaction, was it safe to go there? A place with hunters and snowmobiles? He began listing off every story he'd ever heard (and where he'd been when he'd heard it) that related to anything that sounded like this, this, lodge. He couldn't say the word except as a whisper. There was his old boss who retired to the country and died on a Sunday afternoon, chopping down a tree that then fell on him. Dad was at work when he heard, the next day, at 9:18 a.m., preparing a report for a meeting that was to happen at ten.

There was a co-worker's niece who went on a snowmobile that tipped over and she was paralyzed. Dad was in the parking lot at the end of the day when he heard that horrible news. It ruined his drive home (his voice cracked when he spoke of the drive).

There was the young man, who was a friend of a co-worker's son, who died in a hunting accident. Shot in the back. Apparently the funeral was a sight—so many people that they needed closed-circuit TV so that everyone could see the coffin. He was at the water cooler—he'd never forget—when he heard that. What an awful story it was. His hands shook, a breathlessness exploding across his face. He was filled with equal amounts hungry excitement and paralyzing fear of death.

Oh, and then there was the guy who lived down the street when Dad was a little boy, a man—what was his name?—who went fishing and got tetanus from a rusty hook. A horrible, horrible death.

"Okay, Dad, I get it. You don't want to go to the lodge."

"No, no, it'd be nice to go. It's a nice gift." He flashed the beatific smile he used for the church lobby, for strangers when they asked directions, or for saying thank you for a door held open at a store.

Mom sniffed and walked away. "Nobody ever gets me anything so nice."

"Oh, knock it off, Janet," he snapped.

"Dad, Mom, please. Act however you want when I'm not here, but please don't fight while I'm around. I'm away most of the time now."

"Yes, we know," she said.

"So, if I only see you maybe once every month or two, I'd much rather if you didn't fight when I'm around. There's plenty of time while I'm gone."

"You've got that right," she said.

"Janet. Stop it!" yelled Dad.

"Oh yes, you're so perfect with your fancy gift."

"Mom. Your last birthday. Remember what you asked for?"

She turned away, not fully, just askance, and looked down with a sulk that she tried to mask with a faint Slender-Nation-selling smile. Like a cat or a toddler, she could pretend something was not happening by simply looking away.

"You asked for a blender, and I—"

"Yes. I know. You bought that shiny monstrosity that sits on the counter. Wasting good money. A glass, a spoon, a little water, and a full supply of Slender Nation are all you need to survive and thrive!"

"Mom, please, don't try to sell to me."

"It would do you good. Are you staying for dinner? You could stay over, and we'll go to church tomorrow."

"No, thank you. Please don't change the subject. Would you be happier if I took the blender back? I could donate it somewhere."

"Goodness, no. It's valuable. And who are you, such a big shot throwing away money on something and then saying you're going to give it away? Imagine!"

"Well, you said you don't use it, and I don't want it to sit there and remind you of my wastefulness."

"Of course not. Really, you shouldn't be so sensitive. It's a fine blender. Now, are you staying?"

"No, thank you. I have to get back to Toronto."

"What's so important there?"

"I've things to do."

"What things?"

"My things."

"You should stay and tend to spiritual matters."

"I should go."

As I pulled away she stood in the doorway. Behind her, Dad still held the gift certificate, avidly building his inventory of horrible possibilities it presented.

I sped up the highway to the city that allowed me to be myself and alone. In my apartment I spent the evening slowly plucking chest hairs, one by slow agonizing one, until I was calm, and then I slept deeply until the middle of Sunday morning.

Dad never used the gift certificate. We never had our bonding weekend together, and that's just as well, for what could be revealed that I didn't already know? What joy would there have been? I retrieved the gift certificate from the box with his lists, next to Mom's blender, which she never used either. The expiry date on the gift certificate had long passed, but the blender was good as new.

I dropped the gift certificate in the shredder, which sprang to life with a grinding whine that brought me pleasant relief.

NINETEEN: *"There are far worse things that can happen to you."*

Otterton, 1981—Dad suffered a tremendous breakdown that September, of which I know nothing except rare offhand remarks—"It was awful, pure darkness," and "I was in a place I thought would never end." Beyond these vague references, Dad never spoke of what happened.

He disappeared. Mom said, "He's gone, we move on." It was time to build our new lives in Slender Nation, and then it would be Dad to Lend, then my Dad to Lend became her lover. I was born again, then she was born again too, but the whole time, Dad's absence was the unspoken presence in our house.

Jesus and Slender Nation excited her, and for her this equated to happiness. She hummed "Just as I Am" continually in the house. I lurked in the sidelines, reminding myself to smile, to try to feel good, but I worried about Dad because The Rapture could happen any minute.

We were soon visited by Pastor Haroldson.

When the doorbell rang, Mom put down her pamphlet and stopped humming. She looked distrustfully at the door. "Go to my bedroom window, dear," she said, "and tell me if you see a car outside." I only knew two cars that it could be: Michael's beat-up brown Pontiac or—hope of hopes— Dad's little green Honda. It was neither, just a simple, clean black Chevrolet. She was delighted to see the pastor, flinging open the door and leaning into him breathlessly, greeting him as though he might be Jesus himself. She sat him down in the living room and sent me to make a shake. My hand trembled on the spoon as I stirred. *Pastor Haroldson spoke directly with God.* I was making him a drink that was healthy and nutritious and slimming and The Answer to all Food Crime. I delivered it, still shaking, then sat on the floor staring up in awe, seen and not heard and drinking in everything they said.

"It's not much," said Mom, with a wave of her hand. "But this house will have to do for now. How do you like your Slender Nation?"

"Sorry, my?"

"Your drink."

"Very nice. Thank you. It's good to be in your house, and any house where God lives is His mansion. I think you have a wonderful home."

"Thank you, um, Reverend?"

"Call me Pastor."

"Okay Reverend," she said, completely mishearing in her excitement. He didn't seem to notice or care. I stopped myself from correcting her.

"The Lord makes our homes strong when we work for Him," he said.

"Yes, well, I try. It's tough being alone."

The pastor nodded sagely. His eyes travelled from her to me and back.

He gave hints that she didn't grasp. He wanted me to leave the room, and I was certain that this was so he could repeat to her whatever God had told him—that I was bad, that God did not smile on me, that I was not a True Believer (much as I tried). I stood my ground, silently praying over and over for forgiveness for whatever it was that was wrong with me, fearing I'd be left behind. These fears live on in me today, hidden away only to pop up during power outages or news reports of natural disaster. It was eternal life and death that hung in the balance.

Pastor Haroldson dropped hints. Mom pushed product.

"William," he finally said, "I need to visit with your mother regarding church matters. Would you grant us privacy for a few moments?" He leaned toward her on the couch as he spoke, but kept his eyes locked on me. For a moment he reminded me of a teacher I once had, Mr. Hebtant, and I thought this might be an unforgiveable sin, equating a great minister to a simple teacher.

"Where do you want me to go?" I said, not trying to disrespect him, but hearing insolence in my voice just the same.

"William, that's enough!" said Mom. I was dispatched to the basement. I cowered at the foot of the stairs for a few seconds until my curiosity couldn't bear anymore and I crawled back up, avoiding the fourth step, which always creaked. I opened the door with painstaking slowness and listened.

"...but that's not possible," said Mom in a protesting voice. "It won't work. My husband is gone."

"Do you know where he went?"

After a long silence she said, "Yes I do. He's in a psychiatric hospital. Loony. Always was, but I can see it better now. We need to move on and I only tell you this so you can understand and help us."

"I'm here to help."

"We don't need healing. We need my husband to stay locked up."

My throat was dry. My chin pressed to my chest. I got no relief in discovering they weren't talking about me.

"I'm glad we're saved," she said, hastily adding, "praise the Lord, but I don't think church is right for Keith."

"Jesus will heal all wounds—mind, body, and spirit—and your home cannot know its Christian potential, its full power and prosperity as a house of God's service, until it is healed."

"Pastor, I know you're a man of God, but it's been a lot better since Keith left. I've got this business and my boy, and we both have Jesus now. Things are coming along."

"The psychiatrists and doctors are part of Satan's scientific handiwork. They say mental illness when the truth is demon possession. Jesus will drive those demons away in an instant."

She resisted.

I craned to listen to what I couldn't stand to hear, wounded by the bite of betrayal. Everything was different now. She'd lied, but the lie originated from before she found God. She could not lie anymore; it would be sin.

He cajoled her with phrases, "the narrow road," "the love of our Lord," and "our crosses to bear."

She gave in, agreed to allow the pastor to visit my father, on the condition that the pastor wouldn't mention her "or Billy" to him.

"I will go as part of my community ministry," he said. "Your names will not be spoken." He asked for directions. She must have responded by writing it down, because I heard nothing. I wanted to crawl into the trunk of his car and drive away with him to Dad.

I lingered at the top of the stairs, numbed by the excitement of news about my father and the gravity of that knowledge. Was he chained to the wall? Did they put electrodes on his head? Did he murder someone? I massaged the hurt of the three-month-long lie. She may have been embarrassed, or maybe she was protecting me. But I couldn't be protected from what I didn't know or understand. Nobody can.

Mom and Dad would never understand that it was impossible for me to avoid what they fended off; they wanted The Answer while I wanted to explore, to have five more questions for every answer I received, and this was a horrible weight for me back then because it felt like sin. Jesus was supposed to be The Answer.

I can't say for certain what made her acquiesce to the pastor. The cynic would say she simply wanted the business that resided at the church and would do anything to please him. But I think she really did respect Pastor Haroldson. She saw him as a holy man. She didn't want Dad back, at least not that she admitted, but she wouldn't have wanted to remain alone either and being dumped by Michael may have transported her back to the frame of mind she called "the hunt for a mate."

When the pastor drove off, a fast-moving chain of events began. I imagine Pastor Haroldson arriving on the expansive green campus of Westbrook Psychiatric Hospital, more than seventy miles north of Otterton. I've driven there several times to take in its squat red-brick buildings splayed across treed lawns. In the distance is a forest. The pastor is jovial but formal when he steps inside the institution with a handwritten note from my mother authorizing a visit with my father. Dad sits in a group room, big windows, crowded, but quiet.

The pastor is directed to him. Dad looks up with sad and desperate eyes, the eyes that could only be melancholy or maniacal.

"Keith?" says the pastor. "Keith Oaks?"

Dad nods. The pastor's hand comes forward, warm and gentle, his eyes full of compassion. "I'm here as a missionary. I'm here to tell you of the One who can answer your every question."

Dad's eyes narrow, then brighten. A hungry grin creeps across his face as he learns the gospel, and what it can do for him. The pastor sits with him all afternoon. They pray. Dad is saved. There is unspeakable joy.

For a long week my grasp of time, existence, and homework stood still as I pretended to know nothing. I scoured Mom's notes and papers for a clue to where Dad could be found, even rifling through her underwear drawer, but all I found was a wealth of Slender Nation pamphlets and the Bible she'd been given. It was a week I suppressed every urge to ask about Dad. I feared she would lie and risk going to hell. Overwhelmed with the responsibility of getting us all into heaven, I asked constant forgiveness for all my guilty acts, namely snooping and disobeying Mom by eavesdropping.

At the end of that week, Mom and I arrived at church. It was my third Sunday with Jesus and Mom's second. Dad was already there, waiting in the pew where we'd sat the week before.

"Hello, William," he said, grabbing me in a bear hug. "Praise Jesus it's you." I was too stunned to feel the joy I wanted. He put me down, went to embrace Mom. She shook his hand. We sat together. With him was a large man named Jim. Jim worked at the hospital where Dad stayed. The pastor had signed Dad out on a pass, and Dad was allowed to go on the condition that Jim came along and brought him promptly back to the hospital after the service.

"Dad, where did you come from?" I said, hoping it wasn't a lie to pretend not to know.

"I've been away, son, but Jesus has brought me into his kingdom. Praise the Lord. I come to you from the place where redemption found me. Praise the Lord."

"Praise the Lord," I said. I *knew* my heart wasn't in it, and this hurt. Mom looked away. That hurt too. Everything was hurt, as was everyone in the world of adults, the people who were supposed to know everything. I bruised my thumb in church that day, unaware that I was pinching it.

Like Mom and me before him, Dad was saved. And Mom sold more Slender Nation that day. Soon Pastor Haroldson convinced her that what Jesus wanted was for the family to be together again. She signed a paper. Dad moved home to the basement. I wanted to rejoice, as commanded, but Dad was more mysterious than ever.

What was mortally injured, beginning a long bleed toward slow death, was my belief in the magic world where Dad could make everything better by reappearing, and where everything could be made right by repeating a rote prayer. I wouldn't let go of the hope that this could be resurrected, and I wouldn't let go of the sense that it was my job to fix my parents. Jesus was so busy with them, he didn't have time to make me feel good, much as I prayed for it.

I never learned Dad's diagnosis, though I can imagine what it was. And I don't know what led to his institutionalization. That information will now wait thirty years for release. I have had to accept that I may never know, that there may not be an answer.

I will never know.

TWENTY: *"... solace in the love of God..."*

Toronto, 2001—My own fundamentalism: paper and pain. These bring me peace. Power does not. Power brings a maniacal charge. I felt the tingle of power in the arcade that night, and then again during my moment of being born again, imbued with a surge of love and belonging that didn't last.

The infection of power crept up on me as the Book of the Dead presented its unique frustrations. The technical work, while painstaking, was routine. Flattening, cataloguing, cleaning, and mounting were all skills I had learned in training and through experience. But what I couldn't accept was that phrase that rolled off Berthe's tongue so easily: "There will be gaps."

It was entirely logical, normal for my work, but I found it hard to accept this time. As I worked with brush and tweezers, experimenting with different ways of mounting the scraps, an inner voice called me idiotic. How could I expect this scroll to be intact? There will be gaps. All rational thought told me to accept the breaks in the scroll—hell, I once spent a month restoring three pages from a sixteenth-century manuscript, it was all we had of that volume and those three pages were considered vital—but now suddenly gaps were unpalatable? While Berthe worked in Germany to identify the locations and sizes of the gaps between the scraps, the liquid fire in my stomach rose, and I chewed down more chalky pills. My hands shook.

I began planning the scenario of how I would destroy the Book of the Dead: I'd make it look like an accident: a fire, a spilled bottle of water, a... No, scratch that, take the notoriety and make it certain. Burn it! Set off the alarm! Let me lose my job. I thought about contacting my union rep to ask about this, then thought better of it when I considered how ridiculous I would sound.

When it all became too much, I'd dim the lights, bolt the door, and disappear into my closet to relieve my agony by inflicting hidden welts.

Before long, I began to fantasize about paper cuts.

Berthe's emails kept coming, and our sentiments moved in opposite directions. With each new piece in place on her worktable and each new gap identified, she grew more excited, and I grew more tense.

And people never stopped visiting my lab. I eyed the blender, the shredder, and I forced myself to step away from the table and answer questions politely. When they would finally leave, I'd chew my antacids and distract myself by reading volumes of Dad's lists.

During this time, I was also called upon to fulfill one of my volunteer weekends. Somewhere along the way, a program was started where staff volunteered to work three weekends each year in the children's education program on Saturday mornings. I had signed on when I first started working at the museum, thinking it the right thing to do, but I soon discovered how disabling it was for me to teach children for three hours on a Saturday morning. I wanted to quit the program, but years later, I still hadn't got around to it.

So there I was in Saturday morning camp, the expert who'd teach the kids how to make paper. Twenty-five pairs of eager eyes peering back at me, the bright nerds of their schools, in a program I could only have dreamed of when I was a kid. I bolted from the room, down the hall and up the elevator to my lab.

I ate six antacids, tried to breathe deeply as sweat exploded through every pore, and I struggled to concoct an excuse for my behaviour. My eyes fixed upon Mom's shiny blender. I pulled it down from the shelf and returned calmly to the classroom.

"First thing we need," I said striding back into class, "is something to help us make pulp."

Gumming up that blender with paper shreds and water was gloriously satisfying. I crushed up a couple antacids and mixed those in. The kids were delighted to know that we were making acid-free paper. The planet would live another day.

I returned to my lab feeling briefly peaceful. I tossed the blender in the corner and looked at my worktable.

The climactic moment in each version of the Book of the Dead is when the heart of the deceased is placed on a scale and weighed against a feather. Should the heart prove light, then things promise to go well in the afterlife. A god manipulates the scale—a god to whom many of the Book's incantations are dedicated. The god intercedes on behalf of the deceased, tipping the balance to show the lightness of the heart.

Fragments of this scene stood before me, broken and inexplicable and inlaid with gold. I began to cry. The pain in my stomach had returned.

TWENTY-ONE: *"family history"*

Otterton, early 1982, before and after—Dad never mentioned where William Oaks the First was born, who his parents or siblings were, or what he liked to eat for breakfast. It seemed that Oaks materialized in the wilderness of Canada and, by his hand, from that wilderness emerged a city of industry called Otterton. Any contradiction—like the so-called lies of tour guides and historians—covered up the truth, which only Dad seemed to know and for which I had an endless appetite.

Oaks was my grandmother's grandfather, and he died when her father was a child. At the time of his death, according to Dad, he owned or had an interest in almost all of the businesses in Otterton and was in line to be right hand man to the future Prime Minister. Despite all his wealth and power, he lived modestly. Though he could have built the finest house in town, he chose to leave that to the villains and cheats of Otterton, who were many. His Blue Rock mill would have become the first industrial electric generating station.

"Just think, William. Think of all he could have done. And you have his name!" I swooned at the magic of who we had been, with no eye to the facts of who we'd become.

This was the core of family history, with begrudging footnote mentions of the grief and agonies of various second cousins or great uncles who each would have lived a mighty life but for the enemies and injuries or, perhaps, the true family illness, which was never mentioned. Their tales crescendo in deaths told in stunning detail. Dad's childhood bedtime stories.

The history is told entirely from my grandmother's side and is centred on the one man who bore my name, but also on his evil nemesis—the aforementioned John Franklin whose name adorns so many places in Otterton that the city could be Franklinville. My institutionalized grandfather Anderson, of course, is not part of history.

Dad saw only what he wanted in history, life, and in the God of our household. His Bible was layered. Thin grey lines in its profile marked the touch of his hand. These were the passages he read over and over again, the sections that allegedly spoke of apocalypse, of end times, of Antichrist.

Huge gaps in his reading shone out from bright gilt edges of his Bible, radiant strata unblemished by hand or light that spoke of love, honesty, charity, peace, forgiveness—the noble teachings so easy to speak of, so hard to live by. These complexities were of no concern to Dad.

One Saturday morning when I was eleven, as I pondered my chemistry set and the moisture patterns on the basement wall, Dad came to me eyes agleam. "The news last night reported fires in the streets of Lebanon. It's all here. It's right here." He waved a red pamphlet. "It was all predicted in the Book of Daniel, more than twenty-five-hundred years ago."

I wanted the thrill, but it was elusive. Even when I could, for an odd moment, still convince myself that I was saved, I never welcomed the news that Jesus would soon take us up into the sky. It made me wish for all the things I'd never do—grow up, have a job, drive a car, have a girlfriend. It was infuriating that I hadn't been born in the old days, like Dad, in a time before the world had gone bad. At least then I would have had a chance to live a few years before placing all my hope on catastrophic destruction.

When the timbers of your house are cemented with bullshit, you ignore the smell and hope for the bullshit to hold.

Dad read to me from the pamphlet, tracing his finger over the small print that he'd underlined, double and triple, straight red lines drawn with a ruler. The return of Jesus made me itch as though allergic, and I became deaf to Dad's excited chatter, seeing only his glowing face. It still happens today. All it takes is finding myself alone in a grocery store, with an empty shelf before me, and up from the depths comes the numb terror that The Rapture is here.

"Did you hear me son?"

"Yeah."

"Don't brush this off. When they come for you, you must not take that mark. You never take it."

"I know."

"Just let them kill you. It will be all right."

"I know."

"Jesus loves you."

"I know already."

I walked up the stairs and left him behind in the basement. I caught a bus downtown, where I wandered around the gabled brick houses in the old part of Otterton, praying for The Rapture to never happen, and then for forgiveness for asking such a thing.

I'd been to see the old Oaks family house only once before, with both my parents years ago. It's one of my first memories of them fighting.

"I want to show you, William, your heritage," Dad had said, looking over his shoulder at me. Mom, next to him, sneered as we drove Franklin Street, passing rows and rows of big houses with peaked roofs and dormer windows that looked like they were from picture books, until we came to the biggest one of all, and I was struck dumb at the sight of its turrets, its huge lawn surrounded by a black metal fence. We turned a corner and parked in front of a dark brick house, solid but modest in comparison to its majestic neighbour. "This is it," said Dad. "This is where Granny played when she was little."

"In the castle? Granny had a castle?" I said, still looking through the back window at the mansion we'd passed, not knowing who Granny was, but that she had something to do with me. When Dad said "Granny," I pictured a magical woman with long glowing strands of hair floating all around her.

"No," said Dad, "not that awful place. This house, the brown house. That Franklin place, by the way, is no castle. It's just a gaudy monument to stupidity." I decided that gaudy meant beautiful. Granny suddenly descended a couple pegs; her hair no longer floated.

"For God's sake Keith, how much longer must you waste our bloody time?" Mom yelled. Dad's head dipped, then he turned to her, his face webbed with subtle wrinkles I hadn't seen before. Granny disappeared.

"I just thought it would be nice to show William—"

"Oh, wow, yes, you're so very important because somebody once had a house here. Look at it: old and drafty and the paint's probably full of poison that gives you brain damage. Let's go home. Now!"

Dad tried to resist. "But this is fun, it's education, it's—" his voice trailed off as he started the car and drove home in surly obedience, while she fidgeted with the clasp of her purse, opening and closing it with sharp flicks of her finger. Dad whispered, "It's a nice house. A very good house."

"Hmmmph," she grunted, then turned to me and said, "Your father thinks that dead people and an old house make him a big shot." I giggled until I saw Dad shaking his head. "You're no big shot, Billy," she said, then turned to Dad, "And neither are you." He drove. She fumed. I said nothing.

She yelled at him that night, after I was in bed. "Where you're from doesn't matter one iota. Trivia! Geez. My mother dies and we got a letter and two hundred and seventy bucks. Does that make me worth nothing? Does it? And if you're so special, Keith, where's the money from this super family of yours?"

"Janet, I—"

"Where? Eh? I should've married a real man."

"Enough!" he'd barked. I heard his steps on the stairs to the basement, then nothing.

On my walk that day in the winter of Dad's return, I strode past the historic turrets of the old Franklin house and rounded the corner. Oaks house, with its brown brick, came into view. "There it is," I spoke aloud to nobody, hushed as though announcing the divine. "This is the Oaks house." Three stories high, with double wooden doors, the windows in the doors grated with steel, roof tiles rotting, eaves drooping. I stood in front of it and told myself everything once again. William Oaks was a great lawyer, destined to become a great leader, who died suddenly... I poured out everything Dad had said, in a whisper, mumbling to myself but feeling as though I was standing before an audience, until I ran out of story and was alone on a strange street on a Saturday morning. The story always ended the same. Our wealthy and powerful ancestry somehow left us—without power, money, or anything.

I turned and walked toward the mansion.

"This is where the Franklins lived. They were bastards."

I walked, slowly, around the block that encompassed the Franklin house. It was four floors high, square, with five windows across all four faces and turrets rising, battlement-like, on each corner, poking out into the trees. The house was surrounded by a big yard, tall trees, and a fence of black iron spikes. A metal gate leading to the front door was rusted open. Iron letters above the gate spelled *Cranleigh*.

"If everything had gone the way it should have," I mumbled, mustering a weepy, righteous indignation, "this is where we would live. Those letters would say *Oaks*." I didn't know this for certain, but it made sense. William Oaks was a great and honest lawyer who died young. If Oaks had lived and John Franklin had not been a swindler, then Oaks would have had a great mansion.

Feeling suddenly carefree if not brave, I stepped through the gate, grazing the cold rough iron with my fingertips, and walked up the path. At the door, thirteen mailboxes and doorbells were built into the wall. I rang them all with a quick pass of my hand and sprinted away, stopping at the street corner, where I leaned with both hands on the bars of the fence and waited while I caught my breath. For a moment nothing happened. Finally, an old man in a tattered housecoat opened the door, stepped out into the cold, and looked around like he'd lost something. He muttered and shook his head, then went back inside without noticing me. I reached under the fence and picked up a stone from the edge of the yard. Cold and hefty, I passed it back and forth from hand to hand, staring at the house and its big windows fifty feet away. I tossed the stone straight up in the air, catching it in the same hand each time, feeling its weight, feeling it sting my skin harder and harder until I couldn't feel my palm. I held it in my throwing hand, staring at the house, working up the courage to do something.

I put the stone in my pocket and walked to the downtown library. I walked past house after house built with red bricks. The Oaks and Franklin houses were the only brown brick houses in the whole neighbourhood. The redbrick homes gave way to buildings of grey stone—churches and businesses and old government buildings that called out from another time.

At the base of the library steps I stood clutching the stone in my pocket. Limestone walls, white columns, and grey arches, the library was built to stand a thousand years. It was so different from the little-kid, Mother Goose library at school or the concrete and windowless branch that I would pedal to from Belting Court. The library stood magnificent, a temple, commanding a reverence that I was supposed to give only to God. Dad perched silently on my shoulder as I walked up the steps. His voice trembled in my ear with perilous warning. Even before getting saved, Dad distrusted books, because books were wrong about history. Books were full of mistruths, half-truths, and outright lies.

Inside the heavy wooden door, I followed signs down a marble staircase, running my hands along the smooth walls to a room in the basement: "Archives—City of Otterton, Tuesday–Saturday, 10:00 a.m. – 3:00 p.m." I leaned onto the door and entered the intoxicating smell of old paper, the staid peacefulness of ink and dust. The room was bright—too bright in fact for the material it stored, but they didn't know that and neither did I, yet. My profession continues to evolve.

I walked the rows, steel cabinets, and shelves of leather-bound volumes, paper edges fraying and brown, smelling of must and dust, not knowing where or how to begin. I walked up and down. In the centre of the room, in a corridor that split the aisles of shelves, a man sat alone at a desk making notes in a book. On my fourth pass he called out.

"Can I help you find anything?"

"No. No, thank you."

"Do you know what you're looking for?" Wasn't that the question? Isn't that the question? He had me.

"No. No, I don't." It would have been humiliating if I'd realized how lost I looked. He got up from his desk and approached.

"Why don't you tell me what you want to find?" he said. I broke into an instant sweat.

"I'm William Oaks," I said. "I want to learn about my great-great-grandfather. He was William Oaks too."

"Hi, William Oaks," he said, holding out his hand, "I'm Gerry. I'll help you."

"Okay," I said, forgetting that I should thank him.

Gerry began opening drawers and flipping through cards, tipping his head back to see beneath his glasses as I walked along with him repeating the life and times of William Oaks the First, the great lawyer who died so young. Imaginary Dad sat smiling on my shoulder. Gerry scribbled notes on a piece of paper. His rapid movements showed an alert mind running at a pace that I was not used to in adults. Gerry was unlike my parents or any of my teachers or anyone at church. Adults were usually relics gathering dust, people who'd lived their lives and now wanted to tell you about how it once was.

I grew nervous with each new book or drawer that he opened. We stopped at a stack of atlas-sized leather-bound books. He handed two books to me. I carried these like they were serving trays, Gerry carried three more. We took the books to a table and began to look through city directories, 1860 through 1864.

"What was that house number again?" he said. I told him, unsure if what we were doing was right, eager to know more but wanting only verification of what I already believed.

"I've researched my own family before," said Gerry as his finger traced the columns of addresses, handwritten in black ink, looking for Franklin Street. "There's something about it, makes you feel connected to everyone and everything." Franklin Street couldn't be found. This brought Gerry to seek out an old map, on which they discovered that Franklin, in the 1860s, was called Hilltop Road.

Gerry went back to searching through books. Oaks house didn't appear on Hilltop Road in any of the books. We carried these books back to the shelves and returned with five more. Still, Hilltop Road held no sign of the Oaks family or their home. But the next book did. Eighteen-seventy showed not only listings for Franklin Street, but it showed the house at number eighteen on that street. Resident: Mrs. William Oaks, child Oaks, nine years. Occupation: Widow. Property Owner: John Franklin.

It was the tour of the falls again: Franklin. They got it all wrong.

I was kneeling on a chair when I saw this, shins parallel to the floor, leaning far over the table onto my elbow, mouthing the information as Gerry's finger scrolled across the columns. "What does that mean?" I said.

"The house belonged to Mr. Franklin—he must have had it built, and your ancestors lived there after William Oaks died."

"That's not true. They've got it wrong. William Oaks

built that house. He built it and it was a good house."

"That's not what this tells us. This is really interesting. They—"

I jumped back, nearly toppling my chair, and screamed, "This place is full of lies. You're wrong! You've got it all wrong! I want to go home now." I stomped my foot so hard that the bones in my leg shook. I stopped yelling and felt my own sobs. Embarrassed, I was too proud to leave or look away.

"Okay. Okay, okay, okay. William Oaks, you can go. I'll put the books away—"

"You should burn them."

"We don't do that."

I stood red faced, under the distant but watchful glare of an elderly woman at another table who'd come in while Gerry had been looking these things up for me. She looked at me over the top of her spectacles, from which a beaded chain hung in a pearly arc to her shoulders.

Searching for something to do, something to destroy, I grabbed Gerry's sheet of scribblings and crumpled it. The sound of collapsing paper felt like triumph. I almost threw it away but didn't. Instead I jammed the paper in my pocket, next to the stone, and left. I caught a bus home.

As the bus rolled across the bridge, I looked down into the valley at the highway and the mostly frozen river. A thin line of black water ran through the middle of the white sheet of ice that stretched between the banks. Farther upstream were the hills and Blue Rock Falls, where you could swim in the rapids if you dared. I cracked the window open an inch. The cold air smelled of metal and spray paint, blowing from the west, from the auto plant. When it blew from the east, the air smelled clean or of hay or of manure. The scenery of the world went by. I looked out at the Murphy's Motors car dealership. I knew this place from TV because the owner did the commercials himself. He'd stand on the corner with an umbrella in his hand, whether it was raining or not, and yell out the prices of cars, "Forty-nine dollars down, no interest for three months, it's yours. Come in. Let's talk. We'll deal. We'll deal with you!" He pointed at the camera, straight out from the TV, when he said "you!" I rolled past the exact spot where Murphy made those commercials. A black sign with orange letters repeated the promise "We'll Deal!" Trash strewn at the base of the sign—pop cans and plastic bags blown there by the wind, clinging to the black metal stand—made the place seem so normal even though TV made Murphy, and this place, very important and not just any street corner.

At home, the house was quiet. I made and drank three quick glasses of Slender Nation and went downstairs.

Dad stirred on the couch as I came down the steps.

"William," he mumbled, "where have you been?"

"Nowhere."

He slipped back into snoring. Mom came home late, dropped off by one of her sales recruits from church, happy with the day's business and thanking Jesus for her new friends from church. She reproached Dad for doing nothing all day.

The simple truth of our family history, which lay somewhere between Dad's ardent fantasy and Mom's dismissive meanness, was starting to form.

TWENTY-TWO: *"... from the Bible"*

Otterton, 1982, to Toronto, 2001—One typical night at dinner, which we were commanded by Pastor Haroldson to eat together, Mom said to me, "If you really want to serve Jesus, Billy, you'd bring your friends to church and get them drinking Slender Nation as well."

"It's more important for them to be saved than to drink Slender Nation," countered Dad as he put down his glass. "Slender Nation will not get them included in The Rapture." I sipped slowly. Eating excused me from speaking. Everything I said now had new and dangerous meaning.

"Fat people," said Mom, "have far less of a chance of passing through the eye of the needle."

"Janet, you're misinterpreting scripture."

"It's the word of God. We all must pass through the eye of a needle to get into heaven. You heard the pastor last weekend."

Dad groaned and sipped his drink. She looked at him with a menacing frown, daring him to speak back. She was not cynical. She really believed what she said and, in believing, she would gladly fight him. This often pushed

Dad into resignation. When he did argue with her, the fight would escalate quickly, and the subjects of the fight would quickly dart from one point of contention to the next.

I read the Bible. I started at the beginning and read through to the end and then started over again. If something in a sermon or one of their arguments caught my interest, like the problem of passing through the eye of a needle, I would briefly skip to that section, and then return to where I'd left off.

The Bible seemed to have a different effect on me than everyone else. Reading it would calm me, even as it prompted more questions. Epic stories, mind-twisting parables, science fiction-like wars, not to mention erotic poetry; all would steel me into a trance. Mom, Dad, and Pastor Haroldson would point out answers they found in the Bible, growing more agitated as they did. Pastor Haroldson would yell, scream, and fulminate. Dad would lick his lips at the mere mention of apocalypse or Armageddon. Mom would exult that giving unto Caesar was a commandment of Jesus that was exactly the same as buying a product that would make you look good in a robe.

I thought it was my fault that this made no sense. I was missing something. I kept reading, lost in the ancient stories and, unknown to me at the time, becoming enamoured with old documents.

We'd go to church each week, convening by the front door of the house on Sunday morning from our various haunts. I would wait, Bible in hand, while Mom fluttered about and yelled at Dad. He would eventually lumber upstairs and yell back at her. They'd accuse each other of being possessed by Satan, for lack of displaying the love of Jesus, and I read my Bible and waited, fighting off the helpless sense that something was horribly wrong.

I should have been more concerned with playing kickball and building model airplanes. But, no, instead I was reading Leviticus in the shadow of my parents' mutual hatred, overwhelmed by a disappointment that scared me because being disappointed with salvation was a damnable sin. Pastor Haroldson preached that even the slightest negative thought was worthy of eternal hell.

The power of God unleashed in my parents more nastiness than they could muster on their own. Life became exuberant denunciation, each of them adamant in their rightness.

They would scream all the way to church. Their recriminations rose and rose again, reaching a peak near the entrance to the Hillsview parking lot, and then would suddenly drop off like the end of a symphony as they put on their faces of Christian joy.

The Bible couldn't explain this to me.

"Mom," I said one day, "if we're saved it means that we're happy, right?"

"Yes, Billy. Yes. Yes. Yes!!" She hugged me tight.

"Then why do I feel so sad?"

She released her embrace and looked at me in shock. "That means you've done something wrong, that you aren't right with the Lord. What've you done?"

"Nothing. I—"

"Maybe that's the problem. You're like your father. You're doing nothing. Just stop being sad, okay?"

She stomped off and gave Dad shit for being a bad influence on me, leading me away from God, and making me a navel gazer. Later, after taking Mom to a renewal rally, Dad came to me and said I should be careful what I say to her, "Because she doesn't understand things the way most people do." I kept reading my Bible, and if I read it long enough on any given day, I could fall asleep peacefully.

Berthe reported back ten days before the exhibit was to open. She'd done her work: the numbered pieces now had an order, the spacing was set, the gaps were identified. She sent me seventeen images, each representing one display panel and showing what pieces went where. Not much time for me to finish everything, but manageable. Jackie and Bob were busy writing and editing the text to accompany the mounts and were working with an exhibit planner and a designer to finalize the last details of how the exhibit would tell the story of the Book.

Some of my work was complete: the parts needed to build the display panels were ready—a sandwich of UV-ray blocking glass that would be sealed around the edges. The backing would be an acid-free honeycomb paper, and the fragments would be positioned with a combination of paste and tissue. I had guessed that we would need eighteen mounts, so in the end I would have an extra, just in case.

I was about to lay out the first panel when a glance at my computer showed two emails from Terry, and something lurched in my chest—I so badly wished I could see her. I put everything down and looked at her messages. Both were mass emails, one saying she had an investment offer that couldn't be beat, and the second apologizing because her account had been hacked. As I looked at her name on the screen and thought of everything I wanted to say to her, a VP showed up in my lab. I deleted the messages.

"This is wonderful, what you're doing," he said. "We're getting a lot of interest in this exhibit, so we're going to add a lecture on the scroll for the Monday before opening. Would you be available to participate?"

I didn't think fast enough, said yes out of politeness, and instantly regretted it. It filled me with dread. This would be the second speech of my adult life. The first had been the eulogy.

TWENTY-THREE: *"In 1967 he met Janet Stephen."*

Otterton, 1967, and on to Toronto, 2001—They met in the emergency room. Mom, in the waiting area, her arm in a sling after falling on a small set of stairs. Dad was delivering a letter of complaint, addressed to the hospital's president, about being forced to wait more than one hour when he'd shown up with a bad cold the week before.

According to Mom, Dad walked up to her and said, "Is something wrong?"

According to Dad, the doctors were ignoring the needs of a fine young woman, and he was not going to stand for it. With her consent, he acted on her behalf. After all, if he hadn't stepped in to help her then she might have languished away in that waiting room, God knows, perhaps forever.

She told me she declined his repeated offers for help, but let slip to him, through stilted conversation, that she worked at the high school. I see her annoyed by him, but pleased to receive so much attention. She holds her arm in a way that plays up her injury as she stoically denies both pain and my father.

He began calling her at work, every day at precisely two o'clock, asking her to dinner. She said no eight times until she said yes.

They married.

Dad never spoke about the repeated calls, the first date, or any of their courtship, but he once told me, with a sense of resignation, that on that day in the emergency room, he had seen someone whose life he could make better, and what greater call was there for a man than the improvement of the life of a woman? Where would she be without him?

I stared at their wedding photo after a long day with the Egyptian dead. Dad's smile is wily and wide and brings me to despair. Despite this, he's good looking in a button-down way and strangely confident. As a child I would stare at this same photo and not recognize my parents. Not surprising that a child couldn't imagine his parents as people who existed before him.

I asked Dad about the picture for the first time when I was twelve. He said, "That was on the steps of the Presbyterian church where your great-great-grandfather was once a trustee. It was a fine church in its day, but then they lost their way and aren't in touch with God anymore."

I asked him the same question years later, in my twenties, he gave the same answer.

I asked Mom about the picture when I was still a boy. She said, "The photographer was very expensive, so we only had him there for an hour. It was hectic."

But what happened at your wedding?

"It was a wedding; it's what people do."

Hanging from an old nail on the wall in my lab, the photo reaffirmed my inability to know them. I wanted to see them full of love, hope, compassion, eager and excited for their new lives together, but in wanting this I was suddenly, hopelessly, felled by disappointment.

I stared at Dad's maniacal fervour. He is glowing. *This* woman, marriage, *this* is the answer. *This* is what he's been looking for. It *will* be wonderful.

And in Mom's eyes, slightly askance, I see her trying for happiness, but she's distracted. By what? It's like she's missing out on something, perhaps someone is laughing off-camera, and she wants in on it, or fears she is the object of laughter. She wants so much, doesn't know where to begin; her eye can be drawn in any direction.

They don't look at each other.

"Mom, tell me again about getting married?"

"It's what people do."

"Dad, tell me again about getting married?"

"That was at the Presbyterian church where your great-great grandfather…"

Suddenly charged with adrenaline, in the late-night after hours of the museum, it was time to leave. I splurged on a cab home, where I quickly locked the door and calmed myself by lying naked for a time on what I call the mineral bed. It's a plank construction I built several years ago, six feet long by two feet wide, on which were glued evenly spaced pieces of sharp gravel, with the odd amethyst or quartz thrown in for décor. It's a soothing thousand pinpricks that drain away the senses, but getting up afterward can be a hassle.

I lay there until the seared image of their wedding, their marriage, its hope, confusion, conventions, and disappointments faded away to nothing but the dull sweetness of a good pain.

But the Book of the Dead wouldn't stop haunting me. In daydreams I would rip it to shreds, returning to reality with a startled clenched-fist shudder. At night, on the cusp of sleep, I'd see myself marched before a firing squad, a scrap of hieroglyph-laden papyrus pinned to my chest as a target.

TWENTY-FOUR: *"Bisco is best known as the 1920s home of...Grey Owl, a supposed Indian Chief..."*

Biscotasing, 1920s, 1998—Grey Owl was a fine counterpoint to my family tradition; he invented a delusional history and convinced the world it was true. He dyed his hair and skin, wore a headdress and pelts, and toured the world spreading his message about nature, along with his made-up life story. Grey Owl lived with the knowledge that his history was a lie even as the rest of the world believed.

But in my family, our approach was not only to invent a history but also to believe profoundly in the lie, while the rest of the world didn't care or listen. Which is better —to consciously live a lie in pursuit of a larger, ardent belief, or to unconsciously cling to a lie, for no other reason than vanity, delusion, or fear? If my father ever came to see his real family history, would it have brought him completely undone?

But Grey Owl was also said to have been a notorious drunk, prone to fits of violence, and not much of a father, either.

I've been to Biscotasing twice. The first time, it was

George Anderson who led me there.

After showing George Anderson's file to my father, and perhaps *because* of the way Dad reacted, I needed to discover more about him.

A few years after George Anderson's death, the institution where he died became Lakeshore Psychiatric Hospital. This hospital closed for good in the 1970s. It's a college now, bordered by Lake Ontario and surrounded by an ever-expanding city, but in the years when my grandfather lived there it was a bucolic farm retreat. The hospital graveyard is a lost place, several miles from the campus.

With the help again of an archivist, I explored graveyard records and found that, though my grandfather's grave would likely be unmarked, I would be able to find its general location.

On the Thursday before an Easter long weekend several years before my parents died—after a week of screening phone calls extra diligently, in order not to explain how I couldn't make it home—I took the afternoon off and drove to the graveyard. The day had turned bright after a grey morning of cold and damp. I followed the instructions I'd been given, finding myself at the entrance to a rough, unmarked green lawn surrounded by iron fence. Cars whipped past on the adjacent freeway. The hinge creaked of rusty iron when I pushed the gate, transporting me momentarily back to Otterton and the yard of the Franklin house, but the hand in my pocket found only my phone and a piece of paper, no rock.

I walked back and forth through a corridor of trees and rows of flat headstones, stopping at every marker I found. Most were blank. Of those that had names, none read *George Anderson*. In total, I saw less than one hundred markers, but the records indicated that more than 1500 people were buried there. Slowly, methodically, I worked my way to the area where the archivist said my grandfather lay. It was at the back, near the freeway. The grass was long and brown, earth wet from the spring thaw. The sad hidden beauty of the forgotten dead, sandwiched between highway and scrapyard, affected me in a way I couldn't decipher. Here was my grandfather. He lived sixteen years longer than my father believed. My father never met him. Dad said I'd been deceived.

But I had the papers. And I saw the place. I felt the breeze of spring blowing across my face as the cars raced by and the trucks roared and, next door, old cars were smashed for scrap. I stood in that cacophony of sound and sight: the beautiful gnarl of an old maple backdropped by concrete and random litter, sounds of birds and rustling branches, signs of life in the place of death, the sustained wither of existence in the hard world of steel and cement.

I stood at the lawny grave of my grandfather George Anderson. I craved connection to this ancestor whom nobody would claim, but I couldn't feel him there. I was possessed by a need to drive away. With nothing packed except the clothes I was wearing, I found myself speeding north on the highway.

I drove for more than two hours before I decided, or perhaps discovered, that I was on my way to Bisco to see other family places I'd never been. The highway was bright, almost luminous, as I roared north. I had no plan, but I flung headlong toward my mother's hometown, the place to which she wouldn't return. Other people my age were spending their time and new-found incomes going to cottages and casinos or travelling to exotic parts of the world. I was possessed by the urge to see abandoned places.

I needed to know that Biscotasing really existed.

Somewhere along Highway 400, I had enough presence of mind to buy a map. Though I'd stared at Biscotasing on many maps in many atlases over many years, as far back as I could remember, I'd never considered the physical expanse of land to be covered in getting there.

My dormant romantic notions about Bisco resurfaced, from boyhood readings of Grey Owl and Dad's glassy-eyed renderings of what he imagined the frontier was like. Though Dad had never been there, and Mom barely spoke of the place, Dad often talked of Bisco—waxing poetic about resources, the frontier, and its weather. But, of Grey Owl, he spoke only once.

"A liar of the worst kind, a fugitive lunatic who thought it better to be a half-breed drunk... Madness." From that day onward, Grey Owl's books—the writings of Archie

Belaney—came in and out of our house buried deep in my backpack, and later disguised by hollowed out Bibles.

In my mind, Bisco had been a wonderful and mysterious place, dangerous but playful, and I tried to get that sense from childhood once again as I drove north. I wanted to meet natives, to smell the spruce, to feel history. I was trying, once again, to be reborn.

I didn't have any family in Biscotasing anymore, and if I did they wouldn't have known me. It's a town of gaps, where a handful of people occupy a space that once housed two thousand.

The highway burned through granite hills, skimming the edges of Georgian Bay, and the day darkened. I gassed up and drove on, pulling into Sudbury in darkness. I bought more gas and drove into the night into what looked on the map to be empty wilderness. I passed the time in imaginary conversation with my mother.

"Bisco is a place to be from, Billy. Nobody goes there. There's nothing to see."

"Mom, how did you get to Otterton?"

"I got off the train in Toronto and took a connection to Hamilton. I got on the next bus because it was late and I had nowhere to stay. Otterton is where that bus went. It's that simple. I wanted to go to America, but things didn't work out that way. I should have gone to Buffalo. You could have grown up American. You could have chased all your dreams!"

"But then you wouldn't have met Dad?"

"That's okay; you and I would've found somebody else."

I'd been on the highway eight hours before I turned onto a logging road, just south of the Arctic watershed on Highway 144. I drove on into darkness, delirious, seeing at every turn the staring eyes of animals—surely imagined, but perhaps some were real—and many times imagining steep drop-offs on the sides of the road, but I couldn't know for sure. It was like driving continually uphill, to the top of a strange world. The road spidered and curved, and after an hour I took a left at a small hand-painted sign: *Bisco*.

From that point on, the road was more of a path, treacherous and undermined, on which I crawled, headlights illuminating spruce skeletons, muddy clearcuts, swamp, and granite.

It was after two in the morning when I pulled into a dark, cold Biscotasing. Spring hadn't yet warmed Northern Ontario. The lake was black and the light from the front porch of a general store illuminated chunks of ice crushed up upon the shore. I had the sense that I was in a space between two hills and that there were houses nearby. Exhaustion overtook me. I flipped the seat down, wrapped myself in the solar blanket from the car's emergency kit, and slept.

I awoke to see a face outside my window. The car baked in the sunlight. Soaked in sweat underneath my thermal foil, I thought of Mom at Blue Rock Falls, wrapping herself in a reflector blanket instead of taking in the rays of the sun. I was in Biscotasing, with a headache, stiff legs, and a dry mouth that felt like a hangover, in a car that stank of sleep.

At first I thought it was a child who was looking at me, but when I lurched he began to laugh, and I realized it was an older man, in his sixties, maybe seventies, old enough to be my grandfather.

"Can I help you?" I said, rolling down the window, vexed.

"Don't see what help I'll get from a guy who sleeps in tinfoil." His voice had the rounded inflection of missing teeth. "What's your business?" He showed no expression save mild curiosity.

"I got in very late."

"Uh-huh." It was only then that I realized he was sitting on one of those four-wheel dirt vehicles. He started the motor. I opened the door.

"Can you tell me where the graveyard is?"

He nodded up the hill, shrugging, compressing his neck into goose flesh. With his engine still running, he stared at me without a single blink. I couldn't tell if this was intimidation or custom. He drove away, and I walked up the hill in the direction of his shrug.

Biscotasing was bright and quiet, the surrounding hills a mix of brown branches waiting to bud with the green fuzz of new leaves, and spruce trees rising like crystalline green cones spread across hills of grey and brown cut through by strips of lake. Most houses were rotting and falling down, as was one church. Paint peeled from clapboard. Broken windows loomed. Another church was white and well painted, up on the hillside. Vehicles in various states of disrepair lay in yards. In the odd place were signs of life—a newer car, a house well kept. I found the overgrown cemetery sandwiched between what I later learned was the abandoned schoolhouse and the two houses at the top of the hill that once provided the public services of moonshinery and brothel. The headstones were mostly flat and seemed haphazardly placed. I was still wearing my dress shoes from work. The mud caked into the seams between the soles and the leather sides, and I began to realize that this trip would cost me.

Here is what I found:

> John Stephen
> 1920–1967

> Frances Stephen
> 1921–1972

Nothing more and nothing less, just words and numbers on flat stones, and the stunning realization of what I already knew: they didn't live long. Weeds and grass encroached on the borders. I bent down and cleared away the growth. My hands grew numb in the dirt. I wiped my hands on my pants and walked away, back down the hill toward the water and my car. A fool, I had expected something magical.

I walked the path-like streets, exploring the store that sold cans of food covered in a thick film of dust. The man behind the counter became exasperated by my attempt to purchase a pack of gum, as though the transaction would upset the balance of his world. Next to the store stood a small train stop where, a plaque proclaimed, a large station had once seen two hundred passengers per day, workers coming and going from the mills. The mills had been gone since the thirties, but everywhere stood skeletal remains of a once busy town.

I saw the man with the ATV again, standing next to his machine in front of a woodpile. A woman stood with him. She looked like she was in her sixties—would have been the same age as Uncle Phil. They stared at me as I approached. I said hello, and neither said anything, just a slight nod of recognition from the man.

"How are you today?" I ventured, hoping to convince them to speak.

When I walked up to them the woman said, "What do you want? Why're you here?"

"My mother came from here."

"What's her name?" she demanded.

"Janet. She was Janet Stephen when she lived here."

"Oh yeah." No friendliness came in her recognition.

"Did you know her?"

"Why wouldn't I?"

"What about my grandparents or my uncle Phil?"

"Yeah, yeah. So what's it *you* want?"

"I'm here to see the place, never been before."

"Yeah. I get it. Another one. You all come up here and you're all looking for some kind of dirt. You'd be wise to leave." I paused to consider if a self-effacing joke lay hidden in her posturing.

"Excuse me?" I said.

"You know exactly what I'm talking about. There's nothing for you here so don't be sticking your nose into people's business."

"You knew the Stephens?"

"Oh yeah. Oh so special, just like every goddamn one else." She spat and walked away. The expression on the man by the ATV barely changed, but he stayed with me after she left.

"Your mother lived there," he said. He gestured at an empty lot. "House been gone twenty years."

"They lived right there?"

"Right there." I sensed, for a short moment, the awe that I had sought in the asylum cemetery just yesterday, a shiver of connection.

"I remember her always raking the road in front of their house. Had to be perfect and smooth. Boys in town would come along and skid their bikes through the gravel as soon as she was done. Made her scream. She'd come running out in a huff and rake it all up again." He got onto his machine and roared away up the hill trailing a puff of blue engine smoke.

I walked across the road my mother once raked. The yard, overgrown with weeds, showed no signs of a house. I kicked at the dirt for a moment, sensed I was being watched, and walked away. Suddenly I was my mother, proud and wanting. I walked to the store, head high because in front of my house was the neatest, best-raked road in Bisco.

There, by the train platform that now receives stops by request only, I thought of the unknown Englishman Archie Belaney, who became the mystical native chief Grey Owl, and I thought of my forgotten grandfather, George Anderson, the supposed British nobleman who fooled my grandmother. I saw my grandfather and Grey Owl somehow meeting and challenging each other to a duel on the train platform, taunting each other with hoots and screams. I saw my mother, whisking away to Sudbury to finish her high school, with a secret plan in her head to travel farther south and find a wonderful life, the life that would always elude her.

I was happy for the sadness this gave me. I'd never wanted so badly to be close to her. I called home on the payphone. She answered. "Hi, Mom, how are you?" I said.

"Terrible. Terrible. That is, I would be fine except for your father. We're late again, for church. I need to get there and he's bumbling about."

In the background I heard his seething groan, "I do NOT bumble."

"Yes, well," said, Mom, "it's the normal misery. Are you coming home? We have to leave soon for the Good Friday service. You could join us. Or you can come for the late service? You should. You must. You have to take care of your spiritual life."

"That's just it, Mom, that's what I'm doing. I'm—"

"Are you at church?"

"No, I'm—"

"Then you're ignoring your spiritual life. You—"

"Mom, I'm in Bisco."

"Why?" she said without even registering surprise.

It was the first time I'd even thought about why. "I guess I wanted to see it," I said.

"Well, that should take you a few minutes. Did you pack Slender Nation to take with you? People are praying for you. Jesus loves you."

"No, Mom, I—"

"You can get in your car right now and drive and you'd be here in time for the late service. Do you need me to send you more Slender Nation? People would like to see you. People ask about you. What on earth should I tell them?"

Dad came on the line.

"William, hello, yes, what's this, where are you?"

"He's up north, Keith, keep getting ready."

"North, hmmm. Does your work pay for you to go up there?"

"No, Dad, I'm here because—"

"Can you get a tax deduction? You know, the government will try to take everything they can—"

"Keith get off the phone and get ready. We're late."

"Blast it. Blast you woman."

I hung up, banged the phone on its hook. So quick, so fleeting, so instantly gone was my moment of communion with her. I never told her about it, and I didn't tell Dad of my visit to his father's grave.

At the general store, I bought an overpriced bag of chips and bottle of pop for the road, along with a Biscotasing coffee mug to remind me of the trip.

"People aren't friendly here." I said to the man behind the counter. He shrugged.

My family graveyard tour was over and, as it should be, no answers were found among the dead. I drove away, all the way home to Toronto, stopping only for gas. It took twelve hours. I whipped myself to sleep. Mom's well-raked road had satisfied me, but only for a moment.

TWENTY-FIVE: *"Mom's older brother, Phil, left home..."*

Otterton & Mississauga, 1981—The moment Dad left, Mom and I began eating nothing but Slender Nation. For ten days I became delirious with hunger, and she became delirious with purging our house of all food. Then something magical happened. I stopped wanting food. The hunger went away. The chalky powdery drink really worked. It was a miracle.

And not a moment too soon, because there were problems, the worst of which came on day three of our new life in Slender Nation. I returned home to find, in the garbage cans at the back of the carport where I parked my bike, all of the food that had been in our kitchen and basement freezer. Temptation got me, and I quickly snuck a can opener from the house. Mom found me there a few minutes later. My face was soaked in minestrone soup, straight from a tin I'd retrieved from beneath a package of frozen ground beef, thawing in the heat. She slapped me across the back of the head and ripped the can from my hands. She forced me to spit out the soup. Together we had a good cry, sitting across from each other on the oily concrete, soup drying on my sleeve and chin.

"It's hard, Billy," she said between her tears. "We're alone. We're alone, with nobody to help us but ourselves. We've got to set ourselves free from chemicals and financial constraint as well. Slender Nation is the only way." I vowed to try harder. I really believed in Slender Nation. What could be better than a magic powder that would solve all our problems?

And here we were: ten days gone and liberated! We no longer wanted anything else; hunger was dead. Mom and I clinked our glasses and drank our shakes, morning and night, with shakes packed in thermos bottles for lunch.

Craving Slender Nation became a regular thing, usually every four or five hours. Sometimes I'd wake up in the middle of the night to make a shake and find Mom in the kitchen making one for herself.

I no longer felt weak; I barely felt anything. I was free. Mom taught me how Slender Nation worked, reading from the Slender Nation renewal resources manual. "Food Crimes consist of anything that gets in the way of health and good nutrition. When compared to Slender Nation, virtually all foods constitute a crime." I asked her how I could help in the business.

"Best to leave that to me," she said, "because I've got all the training."

It hurt being left out, but then she hired me to clean the house before renewal rallies. She paid me fifty cents.

"It's a drop in the bucket compared to what we'll make tonight," she'd say as she rubbed the two quarters into my palm.

From the basement, I listened to the rallies as Mom went to work rattling off lines from her sales scripts. One time I heard her say, "My son, Billy, has lost fifteen pounds, from portly to trim."

I had lost only four. Slender Nation had, however, helped me grow taller. The jeans that had been new in the spring were now showing my ankles.

I asked her afterward about her mistake. She said, "It's not a mistake if it supports the truth and gets people to do what's good for them." Though I was not invited to the rallies, I began my habit of always leaving a small amount of homework to do, so that I'd have an honest excuse not to help if she ever asked.

The rallies carried on. Mom gave away many shakes, sold next to nothing, and nobody signed up to sell either. One night I came up from the basement to find her sobbing softly. She looked away and wiped her face.

"Mom, are you okay?"

"I'm fine, Billy. I'm fine." She slapped her hand on the table, gently at first, then harder and harder, beating out each syllable as she rhythmically said, "We're all doing just fine."

The next morning, her sheen of poise and confidence returned. Standing in the middle of the kitchen floor, she read to me the counsel of "SolutionOpportunity

Number Five," from the Slender Nation renewal resource manual:

"Slender Nation is a great way to reconnect with friends and loved ones."

This is how I met Uncle Phil.

Mom made a phone call and said we were coming to visit. Up until then my uncle had been more of a concept, like the American city Detroit where our TV shows came from. I knew of him, and he seemed important, but he was far away. Phil was a name spoken only from time to time.

Phil was the teenage boy in the picture taken with my grandparents in Bisco. This photo, the only one of my mother's family, was taken on a day he left town to return to boarding school. He's a bright-eyed sixteen-year-old with a charming smile and hair that could have belonged to a 1950s pop singer. Mom, a child, looks at the camera with suspicion, unsure of everything, and behind her smile is a looming tantrum.

Phil became a businessman. He had a family and lived near Toronto, in Mississauga. I had no other relatives except Uncle Phil and the aunt and cousins I had through him. Though Dad had many stories of ancestors and distant family long past, living relatives—the kind that breathe and talk and eat, the non-legendary kind—did not exist on his side.

I hadn't considered why we never visited Phil. It was just something we didn't do.

"Phil's very successful you know," Mom said, tapping her purse as we waited in the Greyhound station on a Saturday morning. She winked at me and checked her big pink button, pinned just below her collar. "But when he sees this, he's going to flip! He's already selling computers, so Slender Nation'll be a snap." I carried a scuffed dark brown suitcase full of canisters, cinched shut with a black belt. I held it with two hands as we climbed the stairs into the bus. We looked as though we had enough luggage to go away for a week. The bus driver punched our tickets, looked at the case, and said, "Day trip?" as though we were lying. I wanted to disappear to the back of the bus, but Mom held me in place with her arm on my shoulder as she told the driver about the personal power and life change that was his to claim if he liberated himself from impure foods. Had he ever felt tired? Bloated? Drowsy? Anxious? The man listened for a short time, while I stared at the floor and shifted from foot to foot, arms growing numb from holding the suitcase. Finally he said, "Ma'am, there's people behind you that want to get on the bus. Please take your seat."

I walked to an open seat, staring at the ridges in the floor, avoiding the glares I knew I'd see if I looked up. Mom had drawn too much attention to herself, and it was wrong. "Why'd you do that?" I whispered through gritted teeth as she sat down. "People were waiting—"

"It's my job. It's our job. I can't apologize for that. Stop being squeamish. If you want your destiny, you must claim it!" She spoke loud enough that people turned to look, and I buried my head into the back of the seat in front of me, hands clenched around the handle of the suitcase. Mom said in a loud voice, as though to a willing audience, "So funny, so sensitive. I know what it's like to be like you." Then, louder, she said to someone nearby, "Oh, no, thank you. Everything is fine. He's all right. He's my son, going through a phase you know." I felt a hand rub the back of my neck and reached up to swat it away.

If she'd known what it was to be like me, she'd never have told anyone that she knew what it was like to be like me.

She soon fell asleep, upright in her seat, a small trace of spit passing across the makeup on her chin. The bus was on the highway. I watched the world speed by. After nearly an hour, stopping first in Hamilton, then Burlington, we passed a sign that welcomed us to Oakville. I quietly wished I could live in this place. Each city should have a king, and I would be the rightful king of Oakville. As king, my first ruling would be to change the name to its proper form: Oaksville. The town receded.

At the western edge of Toronto, within distant sight of the CN Tower and the tall bank buildings next to it, the bus sliced away from the expressway onto a bumpy service road to a Texaco, which was also the bus depot. A man stood by the shop window. I craned to get a better look through the tinted glass, trying to recognize my uncle from the picture. Mom awoke with the slowing of the bus. After a startled moment of looking around, she said, "We're here," in a hushed whisper. She jumped from her seat and darted toward the back of the bus, purse in hand, calling over her shoulder, "Don't let him drive away until I'm back. Hold the bus!" She disappeared into the bathroom, pushing past people who were standing up to leave. I lugged the suitcase forward, careful to not bump anyone. I wanted to meet the mysterious Uncle Phil and didn't know that family visits make people weird. I placed the suitcase next to the driver. I stood there, near the open door but still on the bus, for what seemed like forever. I looked everywhere except at the driver and outside where I might see my uncle, wishing for Mom to hurry up. I stepped aside to let an elderly couple exit and three people get on. They handed tickets to the driver with arms that snaked past me as if I wasn't there. The driver stepped past me down the stairs to load a suitcase, and returned. Perhaps Mom was trapped or sick or had escaped through a secret back exit. The passengers and the driver took their seats, and I looked over to see the man who might be Uncle Phil staring, waiting, checking his watch, wondering, no doubt, what had happened to his visitors. I worried he might leave. Finally the driver spoke.

"Son, you've got to sit down or leave the bus. This stop is done and these people want to get to Toronto."

"I know. I know. It's just tha—"

"*I* want to get to Toronto."

"My mother is in the bathroom." The humiliation was paralyzing. The driver shook his head.

"Now? She's in the bathroom now?" he said. "And this is your stop?"

I mumbled an inaudible yes and looked out the door to avoid seeing the other passengers, imagined glares now in plain sight. Nearby the man I hoped was my uncle checked his watch again and began a slow walk toward the bus. If I waved would Uncle Phil recognize me? I took one step down toward the pavement. Uncle Phil saw me but looked confused, and I was too nervous to realize I was not smiling like I was supposed to. I'd already ruined the trip, the sale.

I wished and waited for my mother to emerge from the bus washroom; I looked over again at the man in the parking lot.

Uncle Phil was balding, but the hair he still had was the same red as my mother's. He looked energetic and young for an adult, wearing jeans and a red sweatshirt. I looked at him, looked away, looked back. He was fifteen feet away, staring and smiling but unsure. I heard the smack of the bathroom door and saw my mother. I descended the final two steps, and Mom burst through the bus door behind me. Uncle Phil jumped toward her. "Good to see you, Jan. It's been—"

"A long time, I know, I know," she said, with her arms stretched out. He walked to her in two big steps and gestured as if to hug her, but she put her arms straight and rigid on his shoulder. His hug turned into a lean in her direction, which she accepted with a closed-eye look that verged on a wince, and I wanted desperately to put down the weight of my suitcase but was too transfixed by their dance. It was like meeting an alien; Mom really had a brother, and impossible as it seemed, these two adults had once been kids together.

I kept two hands on the suitcase, looking up at them in their strange half embrace. Phil turned to me and held out his giant hand, and I gasped for air. I'd been holding my breath.

"I knew that had to be you, Billy!" said my uncle. I placed the suitcase down gingerly, staring at it a moment to make sure it didn't fall over. By the time I looked up, Phil had been waiting several seconds with his hand out, and I was overtaken with fear that I'd violated one of the rules of men—that code a boy only discovers by break-ing it—by not shaking my uncle's hand with immediate vigour. When we did shake, Phil's hand devoured mine. He pulled me to him with a firm grip and hugged. I stood idle and inert, then hugged him back tentatively. The bus rumbled away to the service road and into the distance, leaving the three of us in a quiet circle around the old suitcase, while an attendant nearby pumped gas into a Volvo.

"Well," said Mom, "here we are."

Phil grabbed the suitcase and led us to a black car with shiny chrome bumpers. "Must be some pretty important stuff in there!" he said, and I was glad to hear him say this; Slender Nation might be an easy sell if he was already asking. I waited for Mom to respond, but she said nothing, and this made me wonder if maybe it was my job to start the pitch. I stayed quiet.

I watched my uncle from the backseat as he drove— smooth and fast and confident, everything my father was not. "Everyone's away. Lil and the kids are up north," said Phil. He had a big freckle on the side of his face that moved up and down when he smiled. "Billy, your cousins haven't seen you since you were a baby; they'd be amazed to see you now. Jan, sorry they couldn't change things on short notice. I had some work to catch up on, so you gave me a great reason to stay home and get at it."

"North, hmm," she said. "We're looking at getting a place."

"Fantastic. If you want a great realtor, I know just the guy." We turned onto a treed avenue that followed a river, and I stared out at large manicured lawns and big houses.

"Thank you!" said Mom. "Hear that Billy? Just the guy!" She didn't sound right. A strange tone coloured her voice, and along with trying to digest this sudden impossible news that we'd be buying a cottage, I wondered if being polite was different in Mississauga, because otherwise she was making fun of Phil. And if we were going to get a cottage, how would we get there? The car had disappeared with Dad. Mom didn't drive.

She didn't mention Dad being gone, and that was strange because I thought that would be the kind of thing adults talked about.

Uncle Phil's house was five times bigger than any house I'd been to and built into the side of a hill looking over the river toward the distant big buildings in Toronto. He gave Mom a tour while I explored the immaculate place on my own, the smiling photos on the walls, everything so perfect, so desirable, and so alien. I walked down a wide stone-slab stairway with steel railings and found a playroom with every game I had ever heard of—slot racing, model trains, and Atari. Under the TV was a VCR which, up until then, was something I'd only seen in a store window. I fumbled with the games to get them working while, I assumed, Uncle Phil was no doubt being inducted into Slender Nation. An entire wall of the playroom was made of glass. I eventually got the Atari working, playing *Tank* as the gleaming river at the bottom of the lawn reflected sunlight. Each time my tank exploded, I looked out at the lush green and blue, and I never wanted to leave. I played for what seemed mere minutes, switching games, *Tank* to *Space Invaders* to *Asteroids*. I was equally bad at all. This didn't matter because nobody was there to see me lose. I took a break to rest my thumb, sore and cramped from pressing the fire button, saw the clock, and realized two hours had passed. An urgent need to find Mom drew me away. I opened the sliding glass doors and stepped outside. The trees were half bare, and the dry, sweet smell of leaf fires drifted across the yard. Phil and Mom sat on the deck above me, out of sight. Phil did most of the talking and Mom said *Uh-huh* and *Mmm-hmm*. He talked of his business, about the boys playing hockey, about his daughter in ballet, what Lil was up to—had her own small interest in a temp placement agency that was doing well and volunteer work at the hospital.

"And how's Keith?" said Phil. "I was a bit surprised he didn't come with you."

"Oh, you know, just great. Keith is Keith."

"That's good. Say hi to him for me. Maybe we could get to see him next time."

"I will. That would be nice."

This was different. This wasn't stretching truth to help somebody do the right thing. This was a lie, and while I hadn't yet told anyone about Dad being gone, I would never have told anyone he was still around. It didn't occur to me that she knew more about Dad than she let on. No, she was lying, and it was not the good kind of lie that helped sell Slender Nation and showed people how to live better.

I walked slowly up the wooden stairs to the deck, smiling forcefully to hide what I'd heard. I wanted to play video games forever and never return to Otterton. I wanted my cousins to come home and become instant siblings. We'd all live together on the edge of this big city, where you could be anything you wanted. As I reached the top of the stairs, not knowing what to do or say, Mom saw me and moved to stand up. "Well, have we had a great time or what? We've got to hit the road if we want to make our bus." A small tray of food sat between them—crackers and vegetables and sweets—with a small plate of crumbs next to Phil and a clean, empty plate next to her.

"Billy, here, have something," said Phil, holding up the platter.

"Billy," said Mom, "is also fasting with me. He can't have any."

Uncle Phil looked at me as though to verify this, and I looked at Mom, and she nodded sternly then looked away.

"Yes. No thank you, Uncle Phil," I said, inexplicably stomping my foot at the same time. My toe stung and I hoped they didn't see me wince.

Uncle Phil took a square from the plate and bit into it, staring at me with a sad look.

"There's nothing wrong with us," I said, feeling a vehement need to defend my mother's honour.

"Of course not," said Phil, the freckle moving up his face. "You know, Jan, you're welcome to stay as long as you want." I stared at the food, wanting to fix myself a shake so that I wouldn't dive into this Food Crime, but I no longer wanted to abandon Mom for this place. That would make me worse than Dad.

"Are you signing up?" I said, stomping my foot again. Phil looked at me, then Mom, with a polite confused smile, waiting for the punchline. She had her purse on her shoulder as though about to leave. She composed herself with a brush of her hand along the sleeve of her blouse. I breathed in the smoke of burning leaves and waited for an answer.

"Well, yes, Phil, I should explain." She blushed. "Actually, well this is the reason for our visit. I have my own business now too."

"That's great."

They hadn't even discussed it, even though Slender Nation meant everything for us.

Now she made the whole pitch in stuttering spurts, standing on the deck, purse on shoulder, Phil in his seat nibbling on a chocolate square. It went on for nearly half an hour. She explained the world-wide conspiracy of food manufacturers. I stood by her as she blushed, squirmed, and squinted. She was unrecognizable, unformed and flailing, breathlessly prattling about the liberty of discovering pure food, the opportunity to become whole again through nutrition. Only one product made it possible, and we were already on board. He could be too, and he'd be healthier and would make very good money. It was about to take off. All he had to do was sign up right now, and he really needed to sign up today because it was growing so fast he might miss out.

I couldn't tell if my uncle was interested or angry or maybe even blown away by all this information. She sent me to retrieve a canister. I ran to the front door and grabbed the whole suitcase, returning in a lumbering walk. I unbuckled the belt and the case fell open, cans falling out and rolling across the deck. I presented a canister to Phil then scrambled to retrieve the others.

"I knew it would be wrong, would be selfish of me, to be in on this," said Mom in a final flourish of nerve as Phil examined the can, "and not give you the chance to join in as well. What do you think?"

His response was quick. "Well, Jan, that sounds like a great idea, but I just can't take on anything new right now. I'm swamped."

"Yes, sure, but how about Lil?" she said with a sudden surge that might have, to her, felt like confidence.

"I don't think this is her kind of thing. You know, when I look at it—"

"But she'd love it, and she'd be good! She could sell it at the hospital. It would be a chance to turn that volunteer work into some real money. All the patients could use it."

"No thanks, Jan."

"But Phil," her voice switched to a frustrated plea, "this is a real opportunity."

"No thanks." He looked at the canister in his hands for a moment, long enough for me to close the suitcase and cinch the belt. Finally, he said, "My loss, I guess. Hey, we better get you to your bus. What do I owe you for this?" holding up the canister.

"It's on me," she said, regaining the composure she usually showed when speaking of dietary salvation. "Just promise to call me when you finish it, and we'll be sure to get you some more. Lil will love it, and it will help the kids with their sports and dancing and school. Well, we've got to go." She made it sound like he wanted us to stay.

Phil waited with us at the gas station. When the Greyhound pulled in, he shook my hand. "You're a good kid. Come and see your cousins sometime." I thought that maybe I should do that. Phil didn't try to hug Mom, just touched her shoulder. Leaning forward, she kissed him quickly on the cheek, like a bird. She stood tall, the way I'd seen her practice in the mirror, but I could see her disappointment. "Hey, take this Jan," said Phil. He pushed several bills into her hand. "Your next visit is on me." I strained to see how much it was, but she pushed the bills back before I could get a good view.

"I couldn't. We can afford the trip. Things are going great."

"That's good," he said. We climbed the stairs and the door shut behind us with a pneumatic whump.

That was the last I'd see of Uncle Phil until the funeral. When I moved to Toronto after high school, he called me from time to time, offering to drop by, offering to buy me dinner, but I always found a reason to turn him down. Aunt Lil was with him at the funeral. They seemed so graceful, so sad, so bewildered by Hillsview Independent Pentecostal. He wore a black suit. I recognized him by his freckle. She wore a small hat, and as I spoke the eulogy, my eyes were continually drawn toward her. Her eyes told me she thought my heart was broken.

As Mom and I rolled home that fall day in the bus stink of smoky air and floor cleaner, she didn't speak, just sighed every few minutes, staring at the orange upholstery of the seat in front of her. I looked out at houses, factories, orchards, and vineyards along the Lake Ontario shore.

As we pulled into Otterton Station, she announced, "This is how I first arrived here. Thought I was going to Buffalo, to the USA, but instead I got off here. Didn't know any better."

"How'd Uncle Phil end up in Mississauga?"

"It's where he got off the bus, I guess. Phil got a head start because he was older. I'm always playing catch up."

We walked from the station onto St. Andrew's Street in a daze. It was early evening, the sun sinking. Shops on that battered old main street of Otterton were preparing to close as the bars and arcades began to fill. We passed the toy shop where I'd once waited in line to play Atari for a five minute trial. Mom pulled me toward the shop window, pointing at a chemistry set. "Haven't you always wanted one of those?"

"Yeah," I said, surprised, "but Dad says they're too dangerous, that I'll blow the house up or something."

"Dad's not here." She marched inside while I struggled behind her with the suitcase of Slender Nation. She asked the sales clerk for the chemistry set. "The biggest and best one you have." He pulled down a large blue and white box from a high shelf. I heard the clink of glass inside and was instantly delirious. How cool this was. Dad being gone wasn't so bad. When he came back, he would understand, would see my brilliance. I pictured him returning from a wild adventure: hiking, climbing mountains, paddling rivers, sharing tales of triumph and survival. Mom would forgive him, and we'd all be happy. I'd show him, on that great day, my skills as a chemist, and how safe it really was.

"Do lots of experiments," said Mom in the taxi on the way home, as I stared at the huge box in my lap and tried to resist the urge to open it on the spot. I grew nervous whenever we hit a bump in the road and the glass inside clanked together. "That's good stuff for you to learn. It has a future."

At home we made shakes, stirring powder into water, side by side at the kitchen counter. "Billy," she said, "nobody in this world will help you except me. We've got to make it on our own."

The chemistry set would be my refuge for a time, and I didn't give up my interest in science when we joined Hillsview, despite the preachings that all of science was deception and lies. Somehow Dad and I, although trying to follow every last edict of Pastor Haroldson, could still be scientists. Perhaps the pastor would see it as a small vice, the pet sin he would concede in order to keep us from worse.

That was the only taxi Mom and I ever took, and our last Greyhound trip together. On Monday, a muddy orange Maverick appeared in our driveway, its colour barely distinguishable from the rust around the wheel wells. Its rounded triangular side window stared at me, a vacant, half-opened eye. The car was the same age as me.

"I bought it from a man downtown," she said. "It was on his lawn. Steal of a deal. It cost four hundred dollars, and that *included* the licence plates! This is a GM town, we can't be like your Dad and his crappy Honda."

"But you don't drive," I said, failing to point out to her that the Maverick was a Ford, which wouldn't count for much either in our GM town.

"I do *now*." She held up a translucent carbon paper. "It's a learner's permit. As if people should need permission to *learn*. Let's go for a drive."

We lurched backwards out of the driveway, wheeling around to face Belting Court. So began a period of misstep and movement by automobile, lunging and darting with wild mechanical power that filled Mom with a glow that was part nervousness but mostly exhilaration. We barely avoided scrape after scrape, as if by sheer dumb luck or providential design.

She'd accelerate madly toward red lights in order to screech to a halt, and would explode forward with wild enthusiasm when the light turned green. She ignored stop signs with visible disdain, but was perplexed by yield signs which, with their vagueness, would slow her to a crawl, there being nothing firm to react against.

When other drivers honked and yelled in frustration, she'd say to me, "The man said this car was one of the very best. What're they all so *worried* about?"

That we did not die, that she was never pulled over, never had an accident, these are stunning mysteries. Sheer luck and desperate evasions by other drivers kept us safe. Nonetheless, she never went for the final driver's test, which, in the unlikely event of her passing it, would have made her on-road madness slightly more legal. Soon after Dad returned, she stopped driving and the Maverick quietly disappeared, a deal achieved by my father when he promised to drive her wherever she wanted to go, whenever she wanted to go, forever.

TWENTY-SIX: *"My grandmother would often be forced to restrain her."*

Biscotasing, 1950s, Otterton, 1987—Mom would speak in great detail of how she wailed at, slapped, and punched my grandmother, swearing to her face that she'd never be forgiven for holding her back. I believe Mom's life turned on these memory scenes, which always happened when Phil left and Mom was not allowed to go with him.

Her tears never stopped, but went beneath the surface, an underground river. She became a cavern of rage for being left behind. She denied being angry, much as she claimed to never be sad.

Mom told me, monthly, stories of slapping her own mother. The story would change depending on the circumstance that prompted her to tell it. She was either never more honest than the time she slapped and screamed at her mother, or she'd never forgiven herself for slapping her mother, or she showed them she wasn't going to be pushed around, or it was the saddest day of her life, or it was the most exhilarating moment of her life, or she didn't know any better, or what else could she do except hate her parents?

Is there really a past tense for hate? Can you stop hating someone once you've started? When Mom talked about her mother, was she stating present fact or ancient history?

In the black-and-white photo of Mom and her family at the Biscotasing station, I see her life: she is unsure of what's happening, she's been left out, and she'll do anything to find her way in.

Whatever tribe first said it, they got it right: a photo captures part of your soul.

My mother was a world of contradictions, capable of embracing belief yet short on understanding. Any information she acquired would be bent to her purposes or, if unsuitable, summarily dismissed.

When I was seventeen and serving church and Slender Nation only in pantomime so that I wouldn't be kicked out of the house, she declared to me over lunch, "Brilliant people aren't those who see what's there. They're the ones who see what's missing, who see what's coming. If we all work hard enough, we can be like that."

I quietly seethed in a teenage way, which she took as agreement. "One day," she said, "this is going to really take off."

By then, Slender Nation was the largest source of income in our family, which she donated 20 percent of to Hillsview. I didn't share her beliefs. Maybe she saw through me, but wore a disguise just like I did.

TWENTY-SEVEN: *"Mom often spoke of a recurring dream."*

Otterton & Toronto, 2001, Biscotasing, 1950s—During the eulogy, I looked up and momentarily caught Phil's eye. He leaned forward, tearful, and I looked back to my script.

Phil's calls after the funeral never stopped, but I never took them. His message was always the same, "Billy, your uncle Phil here, hope you're well. Please give me a call when you have a chance." Every few days he lit up the red light on my phone.

I finally called him back during the insane week before the Book of the Dead was to go on exhibit. My mounts were not yet complete, I hadn't started writing my speech for the lecture panel at the opening and, feeling overwhelmed, calling Phil seemed like a worthy procrastination in the face of deadlines. We met for coffee in a little place on Queen Street where everybody worked hard to look like they weren't working hard at looking cool. I had an espresso. He sat down and started talking almost immediately—his freckle working up and down with fervour. "That girl on the tracks—from your funeral speech—the girl on the tracks in Bisco. Don't be worrying about that or saying that. It's not her."

"Sorry?"

"The girl by the tracks was not your mother."

"I don't understand."

"That happened before we were born—that story was already around when I was a kid in the forties."

I must have looked at him with abject confusion, because he started talking louder and slower, like a redneck traveller in a foreign country. "The girl on the railroad tracks was not your mother. Don't worry about that kind of thing."

"What—"

"I mean, Billy, I don't believe in ghosts, but that story always got to me. So many people saw her. I would never, even as a teenager, walk along the railroad tracks alone because of her. She wasn't your mom."

My confusion became interest. "Of course not, I know it wasn't," I said, feigning knowledge. "It was just a dream."

"Exactly."

"Perhaps I shouldn't have told that story."

"Oh, hell, don't worry about it. It was a nice touch. You were under a lot of stress and you did a good job."

"The people at the church didn't think so."

"Yeah, well, fuck them." My uncle, it seemed, was more kin to me than I knew. "So, you getting by okay?"

"Yeah, yeah I'm fine. Work keeps me busy."

"What've they got you up to?"

I told him about the Book of the Dead, about Jackie, the cookie tin, Berthe, my speech next week. He listened and nodded as I told him about the hours I was putting in, the deadlines I struggled to meet.

He tapped the table and said, "So, what's your cut? How much do you get?"

"From what?"

"From this exhibit. It's going to bring people in, isn't it?"

"Some. Yeah, sure. I just get paid my salary."

"That's the problem. You got to renegotiate that. You should get a cut. And what about a sideline? There's got to be more hidden treasure in that museum nobody knows about. There's a grey market out there for that, isn't there?"

"You mean a black market."

"Hey, whatever. Just joshing with you." But it seemed he might be deadly serious. "Just saying you should make sure you look after what's yours."

"That's good advice," I said, though it wasn't. "Hey, Phil, why do you think Mom always thought about that girl?" He was more relaxed now, ready to talk.

"Who knows? Your mom always wanted to get away, and the tracks were the way out. That girl was the ghost by the tracks. Like I said, I don't believe in ghosts, but so many people saw her over the years."

"What'd she look like?"

"Everybody says she wore a dress. Most people saw her near dusk, carrying a lantern. The train pulls in and she disappears. I've also heard of people seeing her in daytime, playing by the pine trees, and in that story she yells out as though someone is trying to take her away."

"So who was she?"

"Hard to say. She could've been anyone. Let's face it, things happened up there. Towns like Bisco—isolated and rough—have their skeletons. There are good people everywhere, and Biscotasing was no exception, but you can find more than your share of dangerous people too. The police were far away, you could only get in or out via the tracks. Men came and went almost by the day, working the rails and the mills. It was rough, and we were just kids. We didn't know."

A side of Mom I'd never considered flashed open before me. A new history appeared, a chasm along which I'd been walking in the fog. "Yeah, yeah," I said, carefully. "Things happened, didn't they?" I dreaded learning what things meant.

"Everybody said it was some drifters who came in on a boxcar who got the girl by the tracks, but people always want to say it's someone from out of town when a crime happens in their midst. Maybe it's true, maybe it isn't.

"My parents, especially your grandma, worked hard to watch over your mom, keep her safe and out of trouble. Your mom hated it." He wiped a small tear. His face strained with the effort. "There were good people there, but there were those who weren't. People got hurt."

"You're exaggerating," I said.

"Wish I was." He crossed his hands slowly. "But I don't think so. There's nothing special about the skeletons of that town; every place has skeletons. And the more isolated a place is, the more it operates on its own laws. I didn't catch on when I was younger. I used to like going back there, loved going back to visit. Your mother and I were friends then, stayed that way until she left. Then things changed. Whether it was her or me, I don't know, but she grew cold to me. She had all the reason to resent me. I got out young. I had a chance to find a life for myself before I even knew I was doing so. I loved going back until it dawned on me that things happened that nobody would speak of."

"When did you realize that?"

"After Jeff was born." Jeff was Phil's first son, my older cousin. "As soon as I became a parent, everything about life up there became clear as day." He began to weep. "My folks got me out of there young, but they didn't do that for your mother. That's how it was. Not saying it was right, but that's how it was. Doesn't mean they didn't protect her. Like I said, your grandmother was over her like a hawk, but man how they fought. Maybe they never sent her off to school because they didn't think she'd do anything with herself. I think her whole life was about trying to prove that wrong.

"When I think of Bisco, it's like everything is legend or ghost. It's not even a real place to me anymore. I think of the girl by the tracks, and I wonder if there but for the grace of God... God's a ghost to me—don't believe in him either—but after you hear enough stories you start to wonder.

"I know it's wrong, but I can't help it, whenever I see somebody still living in a place like that I get suspicious; they've got a ghost or two of their own. When the town died, and it was starting to die before I was born, everybody left. Those who stayed behind or arrived after that, they're there for a reason, hiding out from the world or somebody or something."

"Were your parents hiding?"

"No. For all their hard work, my parents had a flaw. They were suckers for believing. They believed things would get better and a new mill would open, or the railway would grow bigger. They might strike gold at their very feet. If they dared to leave, something good might happen in Bisco. They'd miss out and regret it forever."

I thought of Mom and Slender Nation, and Dad waiting for The Rapture.

"Your grandfather made enough to get by on seasonal work, cutting for whoever—Kimberley, Eddy's—and because they could get by, they stayed because maybe things would get better.

"No. They kept to themselves and kept clean. Probably were seen as snobs by the harder locals, which is funny when you consider that my folks never even set foot in a church except for weddings and baptisms."

"Is there a chance that Mom was molested, was raped?" I said. It was unbelievable to be asking.

"I really hope not. But who can say? Who can say? People keep their secrets, and that town had its share. All your mom ever wanted to do was get away. She wanted that from the very beginning. The walls of her room were covered with cutouts from magazines and pictures of the Queen. She was obsessed with royalty and movie stars before she'd ever seen a movie."

And she came to Otterton and married the man who professed himself a local royal.

"When she finally got away, she never went back. I had to bury my parents without her. Maybe," he took a breath, "maybe I could have done something for her. But what? I wish I knew."

"Nothing. Phil. Nothing. What your parents did wasn't your fault." The words shocked me; I'd never said anything like this to anyone before.

"I tried to help." He was crying like a child now. "I tried to give advice, to send money, but she always refused it. I tried to help you—kept asking her if you'd like to visit with us, maybe spend a week at the cottage. She always told me that you didn't want to, that you were too busy, and then when she got into religion, she'd say that you couldn't come stay with us because we weren't born-again and, oh, Christ, whenever we spoke, it always came down to her pushing that goddamned Slender Nation!" He slammed his fist.

Mom was like that. The moment you began to feel for her was the moment you were only a moment away from being enraged by her. I'd never heard of any of these invitations.

"Did you get the gifts I sent you? It would have been nice to get a thank you."

"Gifts?"

"Yeah. You know. Christmas, birthdays, your graduation. I sent you a five-hundred dollar money order when you finished high school and never heard squat from you." I was struck dumb. "Shit," he said, "you never got it. Christ, your mother. I even offered for you to stay with us when you went to university."

It sunk in slowly. My student loans were still hanging over me. She'd kept those gifts from me out of pride, just as she'd refused his offer to pay for our trip all those years ago. But this quickly fell out of my consciousness, replaced with a new fixation on Biscotasing.

Before I left him I said, "Phil, what would you think if I said that my parents killed each other?"

"Well, leave two people alone with each other long enough and anything is possible. You could've left me alone with either one of them and I surely would've gone nuts. I don't know how you did it. I'm sad they're gone. I would've liked to know them better, but the little I got to know of both of 'em, yeah, what you say could be right."

I returned to the lab and worked furiously, all night, my hands moving as if by their own command from one fragment to the next, from paper to paper as I slipped into a swift trance, working on the display panels as my mind walked the rail tracks of my mother's town; a low current of rage ran through me as I contemplated what the town might have done to her.

Papyrus is brittle, and I'm nothing if not careful with my charges, but tonight I was carefree: arranging and mounting with speed and dexterity while compiling notes in my book for my presentation. Multitasking, as they say. My father's lists became my occasional distraction, filling me with drive and purpose. My lab became a glorious mashup of all its accumulations: papyrus and paper, artifacts and keepsakes, family memorabilia and historic document. All were in motion. I was the master. There was so much to do, so much to think about, so much to think about thinking about. I worked into the night.

As morning came, I booked myself a train and a hotel. Yes, there was so much work to do, but I had no choice—I found myself once again heading north.

TWENTY-EIGHT: *"...her attitude was more practical"*

Otterton—Like Dad, Mom lived with the terror of making mistakes. Dad responded by living a moribund and depressed life, doing as little as possible. Mom embraced activities with exuberance. The difference for her was her belief that taking the right path in life ensured that mistakes could not be made. And if she was on a path, she became driven in her belief that it was the right one and defended herself accordingly. When Dad, just before he disappeared, called the then-new Slender Nation "a pyramid scheme of snake-oil selling that targets stupid people," she shouted him down with the righteous vitality of a revival preacher.

The only parts of her life that she didn't defend were her marriage and her hometown. She could, on occasion, give rational reasons for why she was with Dad, but he did not evoke the passion she had for self-improvement, Slender Nation, or Jesus.

I'm reminded of her whenever I read about the interactions that take place in pro sports. A player is a hero in one town and vilified in another. He holds a noon press conference to announce his departure, his new contract, and suddenly the polarities of adulation and hatred are reversed. Everything Mom did was cheering for the home team. I know most people do this, but she took it to levels that terrified me.

Before Jesus and Slender Nation came the other diets: the all-water diet, then the all-cabbage diet, then the time we were only allowed to eat meat. All ended the same. She discovered something lurid and wicked behind those who'd perpetrated these deceptions upon her.

"I should sue!" she would say.

Then the tag team of Christ and the Slender Nation Corporation brought stability to our lives. They were the free agents who signed on and honoured their promise to never leave town.

TWENTY-NINE: *"Biscotasing is a place to be from…"*

Biscotasing, June 2001—On my second trip to Bisco, I moved with slightly more method. Sleep deprived, I again drove at a frantic pace, but this time a train ticket and hotel reservation possessed me of a new confidence. It was Friday morning and I was skipping work after my all-nighter in the lab. The highway was not yet clogged with its snail trail of cottagers in overpacked cars. I would take the train to Bisco and stay one night in a room rented above the general store.

My mother and the girl on the tracks danced around in my mind, while Dad's monotone occasionally interjected with proclamations about the glorious northern wilderness that he'd never seen. When he spoke, Mom and the girl by the tracks jumped up and swatted his voice away.

As I approached Sudbury, metropolis to the people living in Biscotasing, Chapleau, and other Northern Ontario towns, I thought of Mom, a child with movie stars and royalty on her walls. Mom, coming to Sudbury, the big city. She looks around, maybe walks a block or two down by the train station. She takes a simple meal in a diner and considers how to go about finding herself a place to live, but the thought is wiped out by another thought: she's free. Free from Bisco, from her mother, from whatever else. She is free to pursue her dreams, to find all the things she wants in the world. She doesn't know where these things are, but she senses they aren't here, and she's keenly aware that she sticks out: a young woman in a diner eating alone. She finishes her meal and rummages in her purse for the reassuring envelope of money. She pays for her meal, crosses the street with the excited confidence of a debutante, and without even considering another walk around the block, enters the train station to buy herself another ticket. She hopes, prays, feels that this ticket, this destination, will be the one.

I drove past Sudbury, playing over in my mind all the things that had happened in Bisco or may have happened in Bisco. I kept seeing Uncle Phil, his emphatic pleas to me about Mom not being *that girl*. I chewed more chalky pills than usual, the pain a slow fire in my gut. I dreaded what I might find, but I had to do this. I wanted to know for myself the secrets of this town. I wanted to see dirty people and rotten lives. I wanted to know if Phil was entirely wrong about Bisco or entirely right about my mother. Like an alcoholic who knows that he should quit, but still reaches for that drink, I drove on.

In my motel room I reached for my lab notes—my black paperbound book—to begin assembling my speech, but fell asleep instantly with the book on my chest unopened. Still, despite my exhaustion, I slept fitfully. In the morning I drove to Cartier, the last town on the rail line that can be reached by car. The two-car-long train arrived, and I was soon rolling along the Spanish River, passing lakes and spruce trees above which grey herons flew with slow majestic flaps of great wings. I kept my eyes on the landscape, hoping to see moose or bears but saw none, and all I could think of was that I was going to that awful place.

It was near the end of June, hot and clear. I walked to the baggage section of the car, where an open side door let in sweet air. Mom said you can only smell spruce and pine in your lungs. The dread peeled away, but I willed it back; I wouldn't be lulled into seeing Biscotasing for anything but what it was.

The train arrived in Bisco by a causeway that crossed a lake, a glittering sheet of jewels. I disembarked, looked around, and all around me, everywhere, to my astonishment, was activity. The place was teeming. Motorboats came and went with people fishing the lakes. The smell of barbecue mingled with the spruce. Young people, people who could have been me, walked around in the fleece and sandal clothing of campers, loading up canoes and kayaks and heading out onto the water. The dead place I'd seen that Easter weekend was very much alive.

I felt the frustration of unfulfilled rage. I wanted darkness, dirty and menacing. Quickly, I walked up the hill to the cemetery, across the brush to where my grandparents lay, wanting to hate them for raising my mother here, for overprotecting her, or not protecting her, whatever the case had been. I stared at the flat stones that marked their names and dates. All I could hear was the wind in the tall pines, bird calls, and the far-off sound of an outboard engine. The undercurrent of a hot short summer, all the living crammed into that time between the thaw and the freeze.

As in Mom's dream, the wind blew strong, so no insects bothered me. I could see clearly without swatting at my face. I descended from the cemetery, unsettled by this peace, and began to walk the tracks, sucking in the dull smell of baked creosote ties. I wanted to see the girl playing by the pines. Would she come back this evening and carry her lantern along the tracks? But all I felt was free.

My disappointment faded. This place was beautiful. It may have once been awful, but I couldn't find or sense despair. I had no rage to take out upon it. I saw my mother skipping down these tracks, a young girl full of dreams, and there was no bitterness. I saw her alive for the first time, when the world was out there and waiting for her to explore it, if only she could get her chance, and I found comfort in knowing I'd always have this image of her.

I rented a canoe and paddled the lake for the afternoon, returning with sore arms when the sun was low. I grabbed a burger at the chip stand and settled into my room above the general store. I slept peacefully and slept in. When I awoke the wind was blowing again, and the bell was ringing up at the white clapboard church on the hill.

I washed my face, dressed, and walked up the hill. The bells were calming, so unlike Hillsview. I took a seat at the back and listened to the organ and to people singing off-key. I knew that I was welcome there and that I didn't need to do anything but be there. And I was there, and I felt so alive in my own skin in that place.

It was not a return to Jesus for me, and I haven't been back since, but the peace I felt was as real as the love I felt that first night in Hillsview—though this time I didn't leave in fear or craving more; I just walked out the door knowing that I was stepping onto the earth.

At the chip stand I grabbed a fish sandwich. I ate it on the stoop in front of the store. The owner of the store, a guy not much older than me with long hair already greying, swept the front step. I said to him, "This place is stunning, so beautiful. Would you believe that someone could grow up here, leave at age sixteen, and never come back?"

"Yeah. Yeah, I believe it. Happens all the time. Sometimes they show up and tell me they once lived here or one of their parents lived here. I'm not from here. People still call me the new guy because I bought this place two years ago. This is a town that every kid left. I reckon they all had their reasons."

I thanked him and returned to my room. There, finally, in the hours before my train would return me to my car,

I opened my notebook to begin writing my presentation on the Book of the Dead. In my meticulous book of notes and observations, the recordings of my lab work, there, pressed into page after page, were forty-one random fragments of the Book of the Dead.

In my haste to complete all of my work in one night, I'd scrapbooked a twenty-four-hundred-year-old artifact.

THIRTY: *"... the foundation of our family."*

Otterton, 1982—As the winter of Dad's return became spring, we settled into our new routine and my discomfort grew. Our household had a new stasis: dad living on the basement couch behind his curtain shrouds or reading his pamphlets, me in my fort, Mom absorbed with Slender Nation, all of us putting on a bright face for church, and me desperate to fix everything while forbidden to admit anything needed fixing.

One Saturday, not long before Easter, I returned to Otterton Public Library. At the base of the stone steps I retrieved from my pocket a tattered piece of paper, covered in scrawl. I unfolded it, as I had many times before, and looked over Gerry's handwritten notes from my first trip to the archives.

The crinkles, which I'd tried many times to smooth over, had hardened across the sheet like a web. For all the times I'd wanted to shred this paper, I was caught in its strands. I walked up the steps and found my way down the marble staircase. Gerry, the clerk I'd screamed at, seemed to have forgotten me. He paid no heed as he asked me to register before entering the stacks.

"Card catalogue is over there, you'll find birth records and city directories over by—"

"It's okay, thanks. I know what I'm looking for." I said. He looked at me, bemused.

"Go ahead then. Fill your boots."

I didn't know what this meant, but got the suspicion that perhaps he was mocking me. I walked toward the stacks, the sheet directing me to three things that I would've found that other time, had I not stomped out screaming. These were:

> *Otterton Record*, microfilm, May 21, 1864 (wedding).

> *Otterton Record*, microfilm, June 25, 1864 (wedding).

> *Otterton Record*, microfilm, May 17, 1866 (obit).

I walked the rows of shelves lined with boxes of microfilm. I only needed two boxes, as it turned out, because the first two events, the weddings, were so close together in time. After fumbling about at the viewing machine, I finally got the lamp to work and cranked the film over until I realized I'd loaded it backwards. Flustered, I rewound and reloaded, then turned the film slowly forward through time. I calmly read about the two weddings and then loaded the next reel, to learn about a death.

On the 21st of May of this year 1864, at St. Andrew's Presbyterian, by the Rev. J. W. KENWORTHY, Mr John FRANKLIN, to Miss Henrietta STILLS, both of Otterton Junction. Witness Mr. William OAKS, of Blue Rock and Miss Bronwyn STILLS, of Otterton Junction.

On the 25th of June of this year 1864, at St. Andrew's Presbyterian, by the Rev. J. W. KENWORTHY, Mr William OAKS, of Blue Rock, to Miss Bronwyn STILLS, of Otterton Junction. Witness Mr. and Mrs. John FRANKLIN (nee STILLS).

On the 6th of June of this year 1868, at Blue Rock, in tragic accident, William Oaks, Sawyer, husband of Bronwyn (nee Stills), father of Keith. Aged 36. Drowned.

I read these over several times before finally copying them onto a notepad. Then I drew for myself a map of words, full of arrows and exclamation marks. William Oaks (SAWYER—cuts LOGS in a MILL. NOT a LAWYER!) and John Franklin were best friends. They married two sisters.

I thought of what the archivist had said when I first came here: John Franklin had built a house for Mrs. Oaks the widow and her young son Keith. Franklin was no bastard, he was a generous uncle. I rewound the micro-films with slow exacting care, placed them in their boxes, and replaced the boxes where they belonged on the shelf. On the way out, I thanked the clerk, who nodded as I passed.

Outside, on the library steps, the smell of the air seemed new. It was spring air that, like spring air does, made me feel as though I had never felt it before.

I walked home slowly, tracing my way along St. Andrew's Street then stopping on the bridge to see the rush of the river, swollen from the upstream thaw, swirling with rapids and eddies.

A thought consumed me: my great-great-grandfather knew these waters. My namesake, not a lawyer, but a working man who tended the mill, died in this river. I walked on, arriving home near dusk. Mom was out. I made myself a shake.

In my fort, I stared at the pages of the Bible but read nothing. Dad arrived home, probably from driving Mom to wherever she wanted to be. Dad walked down the stairs in gentle, slow, tired steps. He rustled about for a few moments, and then I heard the creak of couch springs as he lay down.

I waited several silent minutes before speaking, enough for Dad to settle, but not enough for him to sleep.

"Dad, tell me again about the first William Oaks."

As he spoke to me through the shrouds, I listened not to his words, words which I knew only too well, but rather to his voice. He told me, once again, of our supposedly great heritage and ancestry, but all I heard were surges and modulations of pride and sadness—a pride that gave Dad liveliness, a pride that made Dad feel worthy, safe, that made him somebody, and a sadness that made him human. I listened to the voice, and it filled me with two opposing feelings. On one side I wanted to confront him with facts, the real facts of our own history. On the other was a new sense of Dad and who he was. What point was there in saying things he wouldn't hear? I couldn't say to him, "Dad, look, here's the truth. It's a beautiful story. See, they took care of us. We were not forgotten, abandoned, or swindled. Something sad happened and people took care of us…"

Dad would only rear up to say I was treacherous, that I got it all wrong, that I was full of lies and desecrating my true history, that this was not what he was taught, that I was a stupid, disrespectful boy.

I listened on, my father talking of the fate of William Oaks the First, the great lawyer, and I cried softly. I stared at *Milling at Blue Rock, 1862*, seeing my great-great-grandfather working the huge blades of the mill, imagining his death. Did he fall into the water by accident? Did he go swimming and get pulled under? Were others there? Did he die alone?

Silence. My father had finished.

"Son, are you there?"

"Yes. Yeah, I'm here."

"Why do you ask? You know your own history as well as I do."

"Yeah. Well, it's just that—"

"What?" For a moment, I considered again lashing out with everything I knew.

"I like the way you tell it," I finally said, a tremor in my voice.

"Maybe one day you'll tell your own son."

Flushed with embarrassment at the thought, I ignored the question this posed: if I ever grew up, got married, had a child—so impossible, really, given the pending Rapture and everything—what history *would* I tell? My father would never know what I knew, and though I felt guilty for knowing it, the guilt couldn't push away the peaceful sadness of a good story about people helping each other. Hope could not be found within my own family; I would need a new one.

THIRTY-ONE: *"...struck the river..."*

Otterton, Spring 1982—I love Easter, when people play the role of Christ, especially if they allow themselves to be whipped. I have no time for those who say that the crucifixion is about saving me from my sins in a real and literal way. I see crucifixion as a lesson on being alive: I must take the pain and the weight and the humiliations of life, accept these as mine, in order that I may live.

After Easter, during that heavy spring when I still sincerely tried to be saved, there was a church picnic, our family's second ever trip to Blue Rock Falls. While I was still fascinated with the falls, the looming picnic tortured me. Bringing church out into the public made me uneasy. The zealous truth shouted within the walls of Hillsview, our house, and our car seemed dangerous as soon as those walls disappeared.

On the morning of the picnic, I lay still in my room, on my back, cocooned in my sheet. The blanket and bedspread were lumped on the floor beside my bed.

In the empty kitchen, I made shakes and packed a picnic lunch—a bottle of water, three plastic cups, three spoons, and a canister of Slender Nation. The church would provide sandwiches for those who didn't partake in the glorious new food.

It was a clear day, but quickly rising heat turned the sky pale and colourless. I went to the basement and picked clothes from the line: white shorts and a shirt with buttons and a collar. I unfolded the ironing board and pressed the shirt, loving the hissing belches of the iron. The shirt warmed me, crisp against my skin. Behind his curtains, Dad stirred. I walked quietly upstairs.

I waited by the front door, reading my Bible, while Mom and then Dad woke up. I kept reading as they nattered at each other. Finally, at eleven o'clock, we rolled out of Belting Court into the sweaty day. In the muted light everything felt different, waiting to fully emerge from the dull, flat sheen. The houses we passed, the cars in the lot at Murphy's Motors, the onramp, the highway, the farm fields outside of town; all waited to burst with light, waited to glow.

Dad had a tape recorder in the car now. Not a real car tape player, but the six button, portable kind. He'd fixed it to the dashboard with thick, grey tape. On the backseat next to me, sat a box of Pastor Haroldson's sermons on cassette.

"Pass me the one from last Sunday," said Dad. This tape was labelled "The Sacred Roles of Women and Men." We listened to this for a few minutes. By the time we passed the old drive-in theatre, the pastor was quoting from Ephesians, "Wives, submit to your husbands as to the Lord. For the husband is the head of the wife as Christ is the head of the church." Mom hit the stop button.

"Garbage," she said. "What about when the husband is completely wrong?"

"Blasphemer," said Dad.

"Then I'll be a blasphemer, whatever. William, give me the tapes." I handed her the box. She picked through it as I watched over her shoulder, settling on "Prosperity for All His Saints." She slapped this into the machine and pressed play with a tap of her finger. The pastor explained how Christians who became rich were the most righteous of all because of the blessings God had bestowed on them. Cows stared at us from a passing field. The pastor's voice died in a moaning lurch. Mom flipped open the machine and pulled out the cassette. Spiraling ribbons of tape streamed from it. "Damn," she said.

"Language!" said Dad. He looked over at the mess of tape in her lap, his lip curling. "You've wrecked it."

"Here, play this one," I said, handing her another cassette. I reached over her shoulder, and to Dad's dismay, she cleared the last bits of broken tape from the machine with a yank. She put the new one in, and they watched the road ahead as Pastor Haroldson spoke about The Rapture. Dad settled into a fiery distant stare, and I began to lose myself in Pastor Haroldson's message.

"As we find ourselves persecuted, as we feel Satan nipping at our heels, as we find ourselves tempted at every turn, it will be then, in those times or, should I say, these very times right now, today, that we must look to Him. It will happen in the twinkling of an eye. The Bible tells us that two will be asleep in a bed, one will be taken and the other will be left..." Mom and Dad, luckily, didn't sleep in the same bed. "Two will be working in the field. One will be taken, the other will be left. People will be driving cars when the trumpet sounds, and I can predict with the authority granted by God that on the day of The Rapture there will be car accidents like you've never before seen. The vehicles of the righteous will be suddenly driverless, the owners swept home to meet Him in the skies. And can you imagine the scene as those vehicles careen out of control and smash into the cars of the unsaved? I won't be surprised that day, but I think those drivers left behind certainly will. How about you? Oh, pray to be among the godly that day, because the roadway carnage will be but the beginning of the horrors. We will be taken up with Him in an instant. Jesus will not set foot on the earth that day, not yet. No, He will descend partway, and we will be caught up to meet Him in the clouds, our earthly flesh transformed into new eternal bodies that cannot die. Jesus will transport us to Heaven, where we will receive our mansions in the sky, from where we will prepare to return with Him exactly seven years later. And what a glorious return that will be!" The cassette player's muffled speaker vibrated with the pastor's shouts. "We will descend with Him, as the army of righteousness, smiting the wicked, healing the nations, and ruling the earth."

"Amen," said Dad.

"Until that glorious day of departure, we who are right with God know that we are each protected, in every moment, awake and asleep, by ten thousand angels personally assigned to us by the Lord."

"Amen," said Mom.

Pastor Haroldson continued on about Armageddon. The blood and the dead and the glorious war. It gave me shivers. Terror and joy unspeakable were so closely linked, shimmering sides of the same blade, it was hard to know which was which. Armageddon would be both awful and wonderful and this was a mystery to me. I said a prayer in case thinking this was sin.

We pulled off the highway, beginning the long winding descent into Blue Rock Falls Conservation Area. A loud ovation ended the sermon. The parking lot was crowded and we were late. Everyone else was already up by the falls. As I emerged from the backseat, Dad grabbed me by the collar of my shirt. With his face pressed to my ear, he said to me again, for the hundredth time, in a whispering growl, "If ever someone comes to you and says you have to take a mark on your hand or forehead—a tattoo with numbers or words—anywhere on your body, you tell them no."

"I know Dad, geez—"

"If they threaten to kill you, let them kill you—"

"I know. I know."

"If they say Mom or I said it's okay to do it, to take that mark, they're lying—"

"I know."

"Don't interrupt me. If they say they've already killed us," his hands shook, "or are going to kill us, don't you worry about it. You must never take that mark. This isn't planning for the long term; this will probably happen sometime this year, maybe even today—you must never take that mark because if you do, you'll go to hell and burn for all of eternity."

"I know." I hated being treated like a little kid, as though I couldn't understand all this stuff for myself. I would have liked to have had faith as well, but when a choice is made because the sole alternative is death, then there is no faith, no understanding, no compassion. There is only fear.

"Jesus loves you," he said.

I ran to catch up with Mom. We were soon in the middle of a group of familiar faces at the base of the falls. Was it right to insist upon being killed for Jesus? Dad caught up with us, huffing. We stood together at the edge of the picnic area. Children played tag (or some other game), adults sat at tables or stood in groups. Pastor Haroldson moved from group to group with Mrs. Haroldson at his side. She never spoke a word.

I stayed at the edge. What was I doing, here with this crowd? If they were already saved, and I was already saved, then my job should be out among the unsaved. But I wasn't saved, couldn't be, and they didn't seem to notice. Mom was already moving about, table to table, saying hi to everyone. I stared at the water, roaring in a glorious fury, far greater, whiter, faster than before. "That's the spring runoff," said Dad. "All the snow melting upstream. It all pours down the river for hundreds of miles. Look at all the power in the water."

"Wonder-working power," I mumbled.

"Or mill-working," said Dad. "Remember that picture, son?" I turned away, walking toward the water.

"Hey, William. Buddy." It was an almost familiar voice. I turned to see Ian Stonehouse.

"Hi," I said. Stone was still a cool guy, and it's not like I wanted friends, but it was good to have someone to talk to.

"Another lame-o church day," he said.

"I don't know. I don't mind so much. I kinda like it here."

"Sure, it's an okay spot, but it's not like we can have any fun with all of these old guys around."

"I'm having fun."

"What, just standing around?"

"Sometimes that's fun for me."

"Whatever. If you like it. I'm going wandering later, you in?"

"Maybe," I said. He walked away.

I took off running, up the path toward the top of the

falls. A hand came down on my shoulder. I turned to see Dad, breathless. He'd run after me. "William, careful," he said.

"I have ten thousand angels with me," I said, speaking the platitude I could not believe.

"You must be careful."

"Keith!" shouted Mom, who'd run after him. "Do not teach unbelief!" Dad turned to her, their frowns met, her words punctuated with a finger pointed at his chest. His hand slackened. I pulled away, up the hill. Behind me I heard their argument fade into the distance.

"You're possessed," said Dad. "Possessed!"

"I am not. I walk with the Lord in prosperity."

I looked back, they faced each other, trading accusations as the Hillsview picnickers pretended not to notice. I ran madly up the hill, dirt clinging to my shoes. Sweat glued my shirt to my skin and it was exhilarating. At the top of the falls, I saw the stepping stones upstream, nearly submerged in the engorged river, but I knew, knew, knew I'd make it as I skipped across like a dancer, landing sure-footed on the far side. I had a few splashes on me but stayed mostly dry. I ran downstream, following the path of the ancient flume, finding my way down the rocks to step onto a perch. The falls were so swollen, so rough, that the flat rock was wet and slick as though it, too, was sweating. Below me, far, far below, Mom and Dad ignored each other, Ian stood nearby being cool, while the picnic dragged on. My parents so badly needed healing. I called out to them. They didn't move. I called again and again, waving my arms over my head. I jumped up and down and shouted, slipped and nearly fell but caught my balance and kept jumping, feet grabbing firm on the slick rock. I was fearless because what was worth fearing? Paralysis from fear was sin. Pastor Haroldson never said this, but it seemed right to me. I hopped up and down and yelled and finally Dad looked up, jumped up, cupped his hands to his mouth, but all I could hear was the roar of the falls. Mom looked at me and then at Dad, and they held each other, their hands intertwined. There it was.

Others noticed me now, but I only had eyes for my parents. Shouts and screams rang out and it was like being saved again. They were watching me; it was love. Quickly, I took off my shoes and emptied my pockets, placing everything on a lone dry spot near the back of the rock. I turned and took three running steps and made a diving leap over the curtain of white jets.

Time and sound were not suspended; I fell for mere seconds, and I heard the roaring boil beneath me as I surfed the air on my belly. I watched my parents, finally in perfect union as they watched me. Around me I felt for the angels, my ten thousand angels. I was torn between wishing my flight and life to be guided within their envelope, safety guaranteed by their magical ministrations, and a simple stark honesty: I couldn't believe. And what angel would watch over a boy who had no faith? I wanted everything: love, protection, triumph.

For a brief moment, I saw my parents just as they were, and I felt love for them in that moment, a love free of need or desire. And still I fell; I knew peace. I hit the water head first.

The cold surface cracked with an explosive sound. All around me, I felt the pressure of water pushing down on my skin. I realized what I'd done and, before making any motion to try to swim, I understood: diving off the falls was very stupid. And, somehow, this stunt was a cousin of sorts to whatever unspeakable thing my father had done.

The icy pressure surrounded me in a mix of light from above and surging burble that pushed me down. I thought of my parents on the shore and how they hoped for a life that would become easy. Life is not easy—one of the few certainties I still believe.

I swam, and I prayed. I prayed to God, even as the existence of God evaporated from my consciousness (or, at least, the God of Hillsview). I offered Hillsview God a deal: I won't bother you anymore if you get me out of this, if I can get to breathe again.

When I found the surface, I was out of breath. My nose bled, and my chest and forehead stung from the slap of cold, but I was alive. Clear of the Blue Rock Death Hole, I was free. Skirting the whirlpool, I drifted downstream in the eddies and walked ashore to the beach, triumphant and shivering. My shirt and shorts clung to me, my right foot bled on top where I must have brushed a rock. I ran to my father, bloodied, exultant, and cold. In the distance behind Dad, Pastor Haroldson led a prayer circle of people on their knees. Mom stood halfway between Dad and the circle, looking unsure whether to run to me or pray with the group.

I met Dad on a bank above the whirlpool. I went to jump in his arms, to feel all the love I had seen in him as I fell. He slapped me broad across the face.

Who could blame him? It stung worse than hitting the water. "You're a stupid, stupid child. You could have died. You could get arrested for that. You should be locked up!" He shook with rage, fists clamped on my arms. I shouldn't have done it, but having done it, I knew instinctively that I'd had to do it. I saw things Dad wouldn't or couldn't see.

Mom ran up and hit me in the chest. In their faces I saw, again, unity, but instead of fear it was now unity in rage. "It's okay, Dad, Mom. It's okay," I said.

The prayer circle broke up. Pastor Haroldson ran toward us, fists in the air, shouting, "It's a miracle!" while others waved their arms to the empty sky. This religion was lunacy. Dad punched my face. My teeth slammed together and I tasted fresh blood on my lip.

"It's NOT okay," Dad yelled.

"Your father's right," said Mom.

I pulled free and turned toward the whirlpool.

If my life and that day could be relived one hundred times, on perhaps fifty or twenty-seven or ninety-nine of those days I would dive in again and never resurface.

But not this day. I stood still, with a bloody smile for the swirling water. I thought about how hard life was. I began my pursuit of survival. Survival trumped honesty. Survive this home. Survive this mandatory religion.

At that moment, I gave up any hope for friendship, hope for love. I became myself, my lonely split self. I'd speak and act a certain way in order to stay fed, clothed, and housed while waiting for a way out. My faith became that one day, one day, I might get away from all this.

Dad's hand came down again, hard. I was ready for it.

THIRTY-TWO: *"...a photo that I took on my eleventh birthday."*

Bisco to Toronto, 2001—In my notebook, none of the pieces from the Book of the Dead appeared to be damaged. None were glued. It stunned me that I'd done this and couldn't remember. But what stunned me most was how momentarily calming they were, how perfect the serenity that came from looking at them. I was guilty of serious professional misconduct. If caught with these I would be fired, and likely arrested for theft. I'd be a laughingstock and yet, much as Bisco was beautiful, so too were the ancient fragments in my book.

At first, the only real shock, beyond that moment of recognition, was the lack of shock. I snapped out of it soon enough.

On the train, I couldn't sit still, paced the aisle constantly, and checked my notebook every few minutes to make sure it was safe. I drove to Toronto from Cartier as the day grew dark. By the time I reached downtown it was eleven o'clock. My museum colleagues, if they hadn't yet been to my lab on Friday or over the weekend, would certainly be there on Monday morning. Our lecture panel was scheduled for seven o'clock Monday night; the exhibit was to open Wednesday. My work should have been finished by now.

I went straight to the museum, dreading what damage I might find in the lab.

What I found at the museum, late Sunday night: The display panels, all eighteen of them (seventeen for the exhibit plus one spare) were laid out on pristine tables, in perfect order. If you didn't step in and look closely, you wouldn't notice that the panels contained a progression of to-do lists, spanning the late 1950s to 2001, punctuated at moments by photographs (my parents' wedding, my mother in Bisco) and other paper items (Slender Nation order sheets, Bible tracts).

In a small, orderly pile at the end of the last table were the remaining scraps of the Book of the Dead, stacked in perfect order. Next to these, wrapped in my leather whip, my mother's blender, plugged in. And sitting inside that blender, perched on top of the blades, was the beautiful gold-leafed scene of the weighing of the heart.

It was all so orderly, methodical, and insane.

I approached the blender as if approaching a bomb, pulled the plug to defuse it, and gingerly tweezed the weighing of the heart from the blender mouth. I placed it down on a work surface, and then removed the whip. It had no place here.

Again I worked all night to restore my efforts of the past two months, forgetting about my speech and hoping only to salvage what I'd done, to mitigate the damage. I retraced my work in frenzied reverse, and by daylight the display panels were re-ordered exactly as before. To my eye, only one piece was damaged, a minor fragment had a small nick, not much bigger than the end of a ballpoint pen. I considered covering up my mistake. Instead, I mounted the fragment next to the piece from which it had broken, with a gap.

I was composing a note to report the damage and the measure I'd taken, when Berthe walked into my lab. I jumped up.

"Sit down. You work too hard!" With graceful steps she walked up and down the length of the panels, humming to herself. I showed her the damaged piece on panel four.

She lolled her head side to side for a moment, took a close look and smiled. "Ya, well, we all leave a mark somewhere, don't we?" I agreed. "What's this?" she said, pointing to the perfect stack of to-do lists, retrieved hours ago from the display panels.

"Just a little project of mine," I said.

"Ready to speak tonight?"

"I will be," I said, with little conviction.

I couldn't spend the rest of the day preparing a speech. Instead my time was devoted to completing the mounts. The fragments were now back in order, but to complete the panels, the top layer of glass still needed to be placed on each mount and then the edges sealed. I procured an assistant—a co-op student working with our metal conservator—to help me with this and by five o'clock we'd managed to complete fifteen panels. The displays were to be moved to the gallery the next day and opened to the public the day after that.

I hadn't slept since waking Sunday morning in Bisco, and in two hours I was to deliver a speech. I considered, for a moment, pulling out the whip, but I needed no pain. I opened my notebook, now clear of all contraband papyrus, and wrote the following:

Speech Notes:

Cookie tin
Gold leaf & Pigment
Fibrous strands
Balancing act of Conservation: Preserve,
but make Available... how?
All documents are *alive*.

With that, I took leave of my lab. After a brief shower in the basement locker room, I had a nap in the staff lounge, feeling loose and easy with the growing confidence that I'd gotten away with the near murder of the most important artifact ever entrusted to me. I woke at six thirty, and went calmly to the auditorium.

It could have been a disaster, but it went well. Speaking to a willing audience, it turns out, is easier than talking with someone because the audience merely listens. My part was a brief five minutes sandwiched in between Jackie and Berthe. I spoke about what I'd done over the past two months, omitting certain details, such as moving much of the scroll to Northern Ontario, getting turned on by the prospect of destroying it all, and creating a gonzo shock art installation of the culminating scene. As per my notes, I did not omit that the scroll was preserved just fine in a cookie tin for a hundred years before I saw it, thank you very much. This garnered a good chuckle. I referred to my work as if finished, as if the exhibit were already complete, even though I'd be returning to the lab to work into the night to seal the final mounts. My closing words were this, "We have to respect the composition, age, and rarity of our artifacts, but we mustn't overly exalt them either. All our documents will be gone one day, like all of us, so it's best to glean what we can from them while we have them. Until they are no more, they are still alive."

This garnered light applause. I was pleased to have not enraged a mob. After the lecture, as I made my way toward the reception that was to follow, a euphoric sense tingled through me. I let this feeling flow unabated as I entered the reception. But the quickly filling room posed a threat: people would want to talk to me. I made to slip away quietly, to preserve that nice buzz, when a hand touched my shoulder. "William," he said, "that was a good speech." I turned around. It was Pastor Haroldson. Behind him stood a shorter man, his face slightly bowed.

I looked closer and recognized him; the blond hair had darkened, thinned, and receded. The lean muscularity had rounded. The cool swagger was deadened, but all the anger was still there. I was looking at Ian Stonehouse, two years older than me, but looking as though life had weathered him hard.

"Ian! Ian Stonehouse. Holy crap. Good to see you!" I said, avidly shaking his hand, delirious with exhaustion and fading adrenaline, but also taken up by the moment of cheap friendship, the fleeting instant intimacy of sudden reunion. To be honest, I was thrilled, still, to have the attention of that kid I'd once wanted to impress. How funny are fantasies; they never go away but instead submerge, reform, and redeliver themselves to us over time.

Yet Ian, like all people associated with Hillsview, was someone I'd worked to avoid ever since the day I jumped the falls.

He and the pastor seemed ill at ease, pleasant and polite, but uncomfortable. The lecture crowd at the Royal Ontario Museum was not their scene.

"Hi," said Ian, with a glancing sheepishness.

"What are you doing here?" I said.

"We want to speak with you," said the pastor, extending his hand. We shook. "Do you have a moment for us?"

The crowd began to grow. "You going to preach at me?" I said.

"It's my day off," said the pastor. Others started to approach—people with questions, there would be endless questions and conversation about scrolls, books, maps.

"Fine," I said, "as long as there's no preaching, hugs, or prayers longer than 'Thanks for the food.'"

"Agreed."

"Let's get out of here, quickly."

We walked together in silence to a pub across the street from the museum, one of those squeaky clean places made to look grimy, where people feel like they're living on the edge as they eat portobello burgers. I ordered a pint of beer, which was rare for me, perhaps a taunt to the abstinence-preaching pastor. He ordered a Coke, and Ian ordered black coffee and a club soda. We sat across from each other. I peeled rinds of paste from my thumb—remnants from the day's work—and avoided looking at them. The pastor spoke first.

"It's good to hear your voice, William, to see that you're well, to see him living in you."

"I'm not into your Jesus."

"I'm not talking about Jesus."

"I'm not my father either, if that's what you mean."

"No. You are William. And you're all that's left of your father and your mother on this earth, but I intend to see them again."

"Don't pitch me on getting saved."

"Not going to."

"Well," I said, "say hi to them for me if you have the opportunity." He smiled, took no bait.

Ian spoke. "I'm sorry," he said with blunt sincerity.

I looked at him. His eyes were withered with shame. It all fell into place. Ian was the guy who'd beat me up in the church parking lot. I was stunned by the recognition.

"Wow," I said, "you really kicked the shit out of me."

"You didn't deserve that," he said with frail voice. "Nobody does."

"You whipped me better than I can whip myself!"

The pastor strained at this, Ian winced. "I'm so sorry," he said. I began to laugh. "Please don't brush this off. I hit you. I held you down and beat you. Nobody deserves that, and to think you'd just lost your parents. That was awful of me. I came here to tell you I'm sorry."

I laughed even more, not at Ian, not at the pastor, not even at this ridiculous mindset that says you can set everything right by saying sorry—you just can't. I laughed because in the face of all the things that had happened, the beating seemed so tiny, so marginal. And likely it was delirium that guided me, perhaps it was perspective on all that had happened, but I laughed even harder, flailing, uncontrollable guttural contractions. I laughed loud, so uncouth, so unbecoming, so attention getting, and I couldn't stop.

And I hadn't laughed since Terry.

When I looked at them, the pastor was near losing his patience, a growing discomfort rippling across his face as he searched for something to say, some way to take charge, and then I saw how hurt Ian looked. He was trying to chuckle, to act like he was going along, a good sport laughing with me, laughing in stride. I saw myself in the arcade all those years ago, trying to laugh with him and his buddy "charging me rent." I reached to the pastor and to Ian, grabbed their hands. "Guys, it's okay, I'm glad you're here. Ian, of course I forgive you. Don't ever lose any sleep over that again. Ever." I *was* moved by his earnestness. Remembering how I had set him up all those years ago, I added, "I think you owed me a shot or two."

"Nobody should ever be hit."

"Let me make you feel better: Camp. When your Dad caught you for booze. He put you in a headlock. That was my fault."

"I broke the rules. I paid."

"How is your father?

"He's dead. Two years. Heart attack."

"I'm sorry to hear."

"He had a hard life."

"And your mom?"

"No clue. She left my life a long time ago. Things were no easier for her. Don't pity anyone; life's better for me since she left, probably for her too. Not sure how I'd handle it if she came back." He took a shaky sip of his coffee. "I take it day by day. I'm staying sober, and I try to see my little girl whenever I can."

"How old?"

"Eight. Her name's Marion." He showed me a picture. Him with a dark-haired, round-faced girl. My childhood thug hero, a doting and tortured Dad.

"Looks like a nice kid."

"Thanks. I have her next weekend. Looking forward to it."

"You should bring her here. Would she like the museum?"

"Not sure if that's our thing. I generally don't leave town with her, coming to the big city can be a bit much."

Feeling I'd overstepped, I sipped my beer, and the bitter taste made me more self-conscious. "I'm sorry Ian, I shouldn't—"

"Don't worry," he said, "my sobriety is my job, not yours. One day at a time."

A silence settled on us. We sipped and stared. Finally, Ian got up. "I need to call my daughter. She goes to bed soon. Pastor, should I meet you at the car?"

"Sure," said the pastor, "you okay?"

"I'm good."

"I'll see you in twenty minutes."

Ian shook my hand and walked away with the lumbering gait of a body that had seen more abuse than I could ever inflict on myself. He was right: I didn't deserve his beating or anyone else's, but he didn't deserve whatever had happened to him.

Pastor Haroldson spoke soon after Ian was out of sight. "That was good of you," he said. "You had no obligation to be kind to him. You handled that well."

"I wasn't *handling* anything."

"You didn't have to be nice to him, but you chose to."

"He made the same choice."

"Well, that's more than many people offer of themselves."

"Is he going to be okay out there?" I said.

"Maybe. Maybe not. If he's not at the car on time, I'll be calling him right away. It's my job to help him find his way, to be his friend in Christ, but part of that is to *not* watch over him every minute. His growth as a person was stunted by life and circumstance, and also partly by choice. He's like anyone else; he needs nurturing, he needs faith and guidance, but he also needs to grow on his own. I'm proud of him for wanting to see you. He's taking responsibility for himself."

The differences between Ian and me, really, were slight; life brutalizes all. What made me different from him was my method for attempting to master the brutality.

"Your speech, son, at the funeral, it was something." I waited for condemnation. "Revelatory," he added, his voice sincere. "I'm trying to be better, maybe that's why I brought Ian here today. You—as your generation would say—you called me out." His preacherliness shed away, an old skin collapsed in a circle around his feet. "You nailed me," he said as a single tear burst, wholly formed, from his eye and ran fast down his face into the corner of his mouth. "You nailed me. Your parents were my congregants, but your father was also my friend. My friend died," he said. "And now my only connections to him are God and you. I've spent enough time talking to God about it; I'm glad to finally talk to you. I heard in that speech how lonely your father was. It was all there and it was true. If Keith had been closer to just one person, if he'd just one close friend, things could have been better for your father. You said it. And if things had gone better for him, their marriage would have had more of a chance, your mother might have been happier." He took a slow sip, seemed surprised by the sweetness of his drink. "I could have been that friend for him, but I wasn't." I tried to gulp my beer, but nothing could pass the dam in my throat. "Don't get me wrong, they got by, all considered, but the tragedy of how they were and how they ended could have been changed. You were talking directly to me that day, and you shook me. It broke me. At Hillsview we talk so much about the love of Jesus, and yet we forget about simple friendships. I should have done more to help them."

I saw the sadness in him, the quiver of another tear that didn't come. He told the truth. He loved my father, and I was filled for the moment with the conflicting happiness that Dad had a friend, and a son's natural jealousy for not being that friend.

"Pastor, I had no—"

"Son, I'm glad I finally got to see you today, got to see you work. I'm pleased to see that you're good at what you do and that you're coping. Anything I can do to help you, I'll do it. I just wish this regret would pass from me, but it lingers. I wonder, constantly now, who else might be suffering? Who can I help?"

I would have, long ago, been cynically amused seeing him like this, and I think I'd have imagined laughing at him, mocking his religion, calling him a leech. I was still half-expecting him to ask me to come back to Jesus and was steadying the nerve to say things that might shock him.

We make choices. I made mine and, though surprised, I meant it.

"Pastor. It's all right. You've helped more people than you'll ever know." For the second time in less than a week, I was in the strange space of comforting another person, and it struck me how isolated I was.

We sat across from each other; he tried not to weep, and succeeded where I failed. He reached out to put an arm on my shoulder, which I accepted.

"I'm doing okay, Pastor."

"That's good. I'm glad to see."

"Not everybody can be awaiting the end of the world."

"I'm not here to preach."

"Sorry, didn't mean to put you on the spot."

"Thank you," he said.

We watched baseball on TV for an inning. I'd never seen anyone so alone. He looked the way I felt. I remembered Dad looking the same. How sad it all was.

For whatever reasons, for whatever motive, for rewards serene or practical, and for whatever results,

Pastor Haroldson had put himself in the service of people who were not able to adjust, who couldn't fit in, who were, in their essence, broken. And we are all broken, each in our own way.

He shook my hand and, wishing me God's blessing, gave me an envelope from inside his jacket. He walked away. I finished my beer. Turning the unopened envelope around and around in my hand, I strode back across the street and signed myself in for after-hours work.

THIRTY-THREE: *"I am not surprised…"*

Otterton—My father liked to play a game called grizzly. I would lie in my bed in the dark after being tucked in. Each time he passed my door I'd call out, "I want the grizzly!" He'd let my anticipation build for longer than I could stand. Finally he'd charge into my room with a roar and tickle me until I was paralyzed with convulsive laughter. He rubbed raw the skin on my chest. I'd scream for him to stop, but he'd carry on, and I would scream louder. Mom would appear in the doorway and give him hell, hands on her hips. We played grizzly night after night. It hurt, but I couldn't stop asking for it.

Mom liked to play snake. I would lie on the couch with her and together we watched TV in the dark, alone, covered in blankets. As episodes of *Dynasty* and *MASH* played out, she'd pull me tight to her, arms wrapped around me from behind, kissing the back of my neck until I started to wriggle. "That's it," she'd whisper. "You're my snake. My big writhing snake!" I'd wriggle all the more. I liked being held, but it was unnerving. I saw how it pleased her, so I said nothing, night after night.

Did my parents love each other? No. Not in a way that I recognize.

They would remind me that Jesus loved me, and they were prompted in church each week to remind each other the same—Jesus loves you. But the words *I love you* may have never been spoken between them.

Did they love me? Yes.

Did I love them? I suppose that doesn't really matter anymore.

I would have liked to love them. But can love exist between people who can't coexist?

They killed each other, slowly, mercilessly, for more than thirty years—a prolonged murder-suicide. Was Dad the perpetrator? In the final moment, yes. For the duration of their marriage, I call it a draw.

They killed each other, and their hopes to save me were nearly my death.

Set aside forced starvation. Set aside attempts to bend my mind and spirit. Set aside how they used me as ammunition against each other. Set aside all the fucked up things they called normal, because I don't mind fucked up things, just don't call them normal. Set it all aside.

I want for them the same romance I felt for Mom's childhood and for George Anderson.

If I could have them back for five minutes and could say only one thing, logic says I should tell them I loved them, but what good could this do?

Would it make more sense to say, "What the fuck were you thinking? Were you thinking at all?" But this, even in the hypothetical, is to speak ill of the departed. Even as I think it, here they are, materializing before me as I stare at the wall. They're forlorn and honest looking, clear eyed, with no trace of the bewilderment they had in life.

They stare at me, and silence hangs between us. Then they speak in slow unison.

"We didn't know," they say with pleading eyes, and I know that this is what people mean when they say, "We tried our best."

I got away, but not unscathed. They did not.

They hid it well. They had to. If they'd shown their rages to the world, it would have meant they weren't right with God. It would have been like selling Slender Nation and being overweight. Their religion was the least weird thing about them.

Here is my hope for their final moments: that their erotic void was finally filled. I see my mother—who long complained that she didn't have what she called "a real man," which for her meant someone who'd defy her—I see her when Dad cranks the wheel on the bridge and looks to her with rapture. She realizes he's really doing it, and she's enthralled, awed, in love, turned on, and about to die.

I see Dad, his whole life bearing the put-downs, burdens, and what-ifs. He's suddenly filled with a sexual charge unlike anything he's ever known. He can't control it and, for once, instead of shrinking from the uncontrollable, he dives in with a full embrace, turning the wheel and hitting the gas with orgiastic glee. For a scintillating moment, having found no ecstasy in living, he finds it in killing and dying. As he sinks into the cold, dark water, his wife dead at his side, it isn't guilt or terror that pins him in place, but transport and joy, the liberty of release. It was all he ever wanted, but he didn't know until then. The moment passes into the permanence of death.

Their lasting union was death in the river where I once tempted the same fate.

I see Dad, washing his little green Honda over and over again, every Saturday. Re-reading each time in detail the instructions on the Simonize bottle, as if they might have changed since last week. He stops several times over the course of the afternoon to read the instructions again. His final moments, so violent, were the only conscious and true expression he ever made of himself.

I see Mom, having just discovered Slender Nation, putting on that big pink button, "Ask Me How to Lose Weight!" and in her smile I see what she hopes and prays is the smile of confidence, a winner.

And I regret wanting to reunite them all those years ago. I should have let them be.

THIRTY-FOUR: *"May they rest in peace."*

Toronto, June 2001—In the safety of my lab—a brightly lit space in the otherwise dark and quiet of the museum—I opened the envelope the pastor had given me. Time worn, and with a new scuff from the scuffle with Ian, was the picture I snapped in the car on the way home from Blue Rock Falls. The windshield reflects the flash, and you can see the outline of my face from the backseat. Mom smirks. Dad's hands are in fists on the wheel, fists so tight because something is breaking.

I stared at this for nearly an hour before placing it in a safe spot at the back of my table.

Two mounts sat waiting to be sealed. The spare—the eighteenth—sat in its respective parts at the back of the room. Everything had to be finished tonight. Tomorrow everything would be moved to the gallery.

I worked carefully, preparing to seal the mount that held the scene of the weighing of the heart.

I stopped. The weight of my parents' lives was too real, and whether this happened because of the scene I was working on, or whether it was inevitable, I can't say. I stepped back, caught my breath, and set aside the

Book of the Dead.

Into the shredder I put all of Dad's to-do lists except two and all of Mom's Slender Nation paraphernalia except her button. Into the shredder went their wedding picture with Mom's confused seed of disappointment and Dad's maniac grin. I broke the picture frame into pieces. From the shredder, a handful of pieces went into the blender, with water and three chewed up antacids; I needed acid-free pulp.

I pulled out the parts of the spare mount and began my extra work.

When I left the museum sometime after four in the morning, I carried under my arm a mounting of documents. Sandwiched between the glass, from left to right: my father's to-do list from the day I was born, the photo of my parents in the car, and my mother's Slender Nation button. Blurring across the honeycomb paper backing, like a cloud, is homemade paper from the pulp of everything else. I tested it; it was acid-free thanks to the addition of my chewed up pills. A little spit wouldn't hurt.

The mount was light under my arm as I wandered into Avenue Road, light of traffic in the wee hours, and for a moment the city was still.

Back in the lab, waiting for gallery installation, the final panels lay flat, complete. They'd be displayed only two months, then put back into storage to protect them from exposure to light, not likely to be seen again by the public for many years. If you saw the exhibit, or if you see it in the future, you may notice an ever so slight discolouration on the final panel, not far from the scale that weighs the heart. It's as though something lightly bleeds through the backing in one of the gaps. The pulp of an unknown paper might be found there. My father would have liked his record to be in a museum; my mother would be thrilled to be enshrined in a venue with royal charter. If you go to the museum and see those mysterious hieroglyphs pressed into the vacuum of their glass sandwich, take a good look and know that the dead are there, along with Slender Nation and the apocalypse and The Rapture and many lists of things to do, fused and synthesized. If you look closely, in the backing paper to the Book of the Dead, in an airtight case displayed in a beautiful hall in a stately building, lie remains from the first artifact collection I ever destroyed.

It's just paper, retired from service.

Out on the street, as I looked for a cab and the eastern sky grew light, there was no hint of pain in my stomach.

In my hand was a small envelope, addressed to Pastor Haroldson, no return address. I dropped it in a mailbox. He would open it to find one of Dad's lists, a special one, a list with jotting in the margin: "Say thank you to Pastor Haroldson. He's a good man, a blessing."

I'd had reasons for everything I'd done. I just didn't know them.

There was more to my inheritance than my father's deluded history, more too than my mother's willful denials and beliefs. I couldn't leave them behind. They live on, popping up in moments, sometimes alone, sometimes fused. I try to keep them visible, on display. Moments pass.

Rest in peace. They never had it in life.

My thoughts turned to Terry. She'd been good to me. She was gone, long gone, and I knew it, but I was grateful for her. She brought me closer to the world; she erased many of my fears.

I turned the corner and walked the empty street, my feet weightless. The air was sweet in my lungs, and I looked around for pine trees somewhere in all that concrete.

— END —

ACKNOWLEDGEMENTS

Eulogy was written in fits and starts, and fits, over a period of many years, beginning with the combination of a short story that I brought to the Moosemeat Writers Group in Toronto in 2004 and an assignment in Kelli Deeth's creative writing class at the School of Continuing Studies at the University of Toronto. The eleven years spanning that beginning and this publication have been a time of change, adventure, and upheaval. I've switched careers and also moved several times, living in Toronto, New York, Haliburton, and Belleville, en route to finding home in Prince Edward County, Ontario.

The writing of this book was generously assisted by the support of the Toronto Arts Council and the School of Continuing Studies at the University of Toronto through the Marina Nemat Award and the Penguin Random House of Canada Student Award for Fiction.

At Tightrope Books, Heather Wood and Deanna Janovski worked diligently to put this book together, and I am also thankful to Jim Nason for boldly choosing to publish *Eulogy*, and to Marnie Woodrow for her sage reading and advice.

I am grateful for the representation of Wendy Strothman and Lauren MacLeod of The Strothman Agency.

Benjamin Taylor of The New School has been a great friend with his advice, encouragement, and unfailing advocacy.

Thanks to my parents, David and Phyllis Murray, who did the most loving thing parents can do: support my efforts even when the things I do only make sense to me (and often, barely so).

Thanks to my brother Gord, who, many years ago when I told him I wanted to dedicate more time to writing, said the words that always matter, "That's a good idea," and also to Steph, Aidan, Naomi, Evan, and Madeline for keeping things lively whenever we visit.

Thanks to Emma and her family—Maureen and Fred, Matt and Kellie, Jamie and Barb and the girls. In everything you've brought to my life, I am the lucky one.

While this is a work of fiction, some grounding in research and fact was needed and generously provided by John Court and Ed Janiszewski of the Friends of the CAMH Archives and my friend Dr. Mateusz Zurowski of the University Health Network.

Thanks to Dan Rahimi who showed me how the Book of the Dead exhibit was prepared at the ROM and, unbeknownst to either of us at the time, precipitated my discovery of the right profession for William Oaks, and added a whole new dimension to this story.

When I needed to find a near-deserted Ontario town, Gail Martin was helpful, generous, and kind.

There are many people who've helped with this book. As I name names, I do so with the knowledge that I am also leaving people out. To my friends, teachers, colleagues, family, and especially to my students, I say thank you; your energy is infectious and generative. In addition to those already mentioned, I thank: Jeffery Allen, Shaughnessy Bishop-Stall, Ed Brown, Elizabeth Bull, Valerie Campbell, Wendy Campbell, Jonathan Dee, David Gilmour, Lee Gowan, Catherine Graham, Dominic Jaikaran, Michelle MacAleese, Thomas Mallon, Mike Matisko, Patrick McGrath, Grace O'Connell, Catherine O'Toole, David Palmer, Angela Patrinos, Ray Robertson, John Rose, Jeremy Sale, Nory Siberry, Laura Stokes, Jackson Taylor, Steve Yarbrough, and Bill Zaget.

Beyond those named here and those forgotten, there are also billions of people on our planet who have not interfered in any way with the writing of this book. For this co-existence, for the freedom of expression, I am grateful.

Ken Murray
    Prince Edward County
    May 2015

ABOUT THE AUTHOR

Ken Murray lives in Prince Edward County, Ontario. He teaches creative writing at Haliburton School of the Arts and at the School of Continuing Studies at the University of Toronto. He is a volunteer broadcaster in community radio and dabbles in several sports. *Eulogy* is his first novel.

For more information visit kenmurray.ca.